# SPENCER

## Fire Lake – Book 4

## M. Tasia

# ALSO BY M. TASIA

## The Boys of Brighton series

*Gabe*

*Sam's Soldiers*

*Rick's Bear*

*Jesse*

*Coop*

*Travis*

*Grady*

*Vincent*

*Shadow*

*The Holidays*

## The Gates series

*Saint*

*Finn*

*James*

*Joey*

*Bradley*

*Carlos*

*Sawyer*

*Trey*

## Fire Lake series

*Brick*

*Fletcher*

*Shaw*

# READERS ARE WILD ABOUT FIRE LAKE

*"What a great beginning to a series! Brick and Roman are perfect together. Add in the murder factor and some well trained military men and you have the makings of an awesome series. It was a well written story that kept me engaged from the first page. Cannot wait for Fletch, Spencer, and Shaw's book."*
~I Love Books 2005 on Brick

*"Fletcher is the latest in M. Tasia's Fire Lake series, a lineup of action-packed M/M romances that I LOVE. Fletcher Daniels is a retired Navy SEAL - handsome, brave, and loyal to the military brothers with whom he has formed a security company, and he finds himself drawn to the local sheriff. Elias Cooper is as sexy as he is protective, and he wants Fletch just as much. Just when they decide to see where this burning attraction will lead them, the new couple, along with Brick and the other guys, become immersed in a missing persons case that hits really close to home. Fletch and Elias are equally strong, passionate men with their own demons, and it makes them one hell of a fierce couple. The respect with which Tasia treats these super steamy love stories gives me all the feels, and those heart-tugging aww moments, the sexy bits, and the suspense make it REALLY difficult for me to wait for the next installment. Once again, such amazing work, M. Tasia!"*
~Shannon Williams on Fletcher

*"I am really enjoying this series and I look forward to more books to come. I like the nature of these stories. A suspense story along with a romance. I like that the romances are low angst and missing the usual miscommunication or martyr tropes a lot of suspense romances seem to have. I think this author may have created a new sub-genre...a light and fluffy suspense romance if that's possible! The suspense part of the story has enough intrigue to keep you*

*guessing and the teensiest bit anxious while the romance part of the story is pretty instalove and mostly smooth sailing without cliched complications. We get a loving, caring relationship that we see gradually develop into more. The emotions are always a key part of the developing relationships helping us to see the men. We have new characters added in this book so I look forward to seeing how they fit in with the group and what their stories are. Looking forward to the next book".*
~Beth I-L on Shaw

## EVERYONE LOVES THE BOYS OF BRIGHTON

*"I loved this book and I love this town. I hope there's going to be more."*
—Melissa Lemons on *Gabe*

*"An amazing read that was filled with lust, love, crazy hot sex, danger, action and so much more This is the first book I have read in this series but I will definitely be reading more in the future."*
—Gay Book Reviews on *Sam's Soldiers*

*"I was crazy impressed that the author made me teary over the ending of a relationship that I shouldn't have even been invested in. I didn't yet know these characters yet the author made me hurt for them. That takes some mad writing skills!"*
—Love Bytes Reviews

*"Jesse and Royce together have my heart. Jesse has it all by himself."*
—The Book Junkie Reads on *Jesse*

*"So much action, intrigue, drama and angst for the long awaited story of Grady and Ben. This was worth the wait. Sexy and sweet. I can't wait for the next."*
—SamD on *Grady*

*"I knew this one would be my favorite to date! There was something about Vincent that said awesome then came Tristan."*
—Booky on *Vincent*

*"This installment of the Boys of Brighton was so good! I loved Shadow and Randy 's story I was hooked from the first page to the last. This book was definitely worth the wait!"*
—AG on *Shadow*

*"I have loved this series from the very first story and this holiday novella is simply perfect. We get a glimpse of all our couples and what is happening in their lives while the holidays explode around them. I cannot wait for more!"*
—bookobsessed on *The Holidays*

## ANOTHER BIG LOVE – THE GATES

*"Ms. Tasia has done it again! This is Saint's story, for readers of the Brighton Boys, you'll know he needs a break! After being forced to become a plastic surgeon by his father, he rebels by assisting people in 3rd world countries, which puts him in the position to be kidnapped and tortured. You really feel for him, that's for sure! Max is the perfect man for poor Saint's battered soul, not that he doesn't have his own issues! Overall, this was engaging, steady paced and chock full of all the feels!"*
—Avid Reader on *Saint*

*"Finn and Miguel stole my heart. This is a great Sunday afternoon read. Finn's character jumped off the page as his story developed through each chapter. I loved reading his truth and watching him and Miguel find their home in each other."*
—K.A. Brown on *Finn*

*"This is really a great series and I def recommend it. I loved James and Ross, it was a rough start for the two, but they worked it out. I can't wait for more, love everything M. TASIA writes!"*
—TammyKay on *James*

*"I may have my new favorite book couple of the series. Joey and Sam just have that something special. At one point I was ugly crying but it was a good ugly cry if that makes any sense. I really love the series and I can't wait for her next installment!!"*
—Vine Voice on *Joey*

*"This author is really talented and I love her series, this one and the Boys of Brighton. Her characters are so well drawn and I can really get into the stories. I especially loved Eric in this particular book. I'm hoping Clay the rookie will be the next book. Keep 'em coming!"*
—Rosemary on *Bradley*

*"Two men with damaged souls come together and find love. A tried and true formula that works well here, especially when working with two lovable characters like Carlos and Clay. Carlos especially was interesting to me - the contrast of his appearance to his gentle nature, a true gentle giant. And Clay being all protective of the much larger, but more gentle man - so sweet! I really liked this story and am looking forward to more of The Gates now."*
—Valeen on *Carlos*

*"Sawyer is the newest addition to The Gates series. The book is very emotional, sweet, funny, romantic, and these two are great together. I look forward to every book in this series."*
—Elaine Gray on *Sawyer*

*"This book has all the feels and pulls the reader right in. It was wonderful to see how the two of them went from adversaries to respect to falling in love. You won't want to miss their story to see the path they travel and if there is a HEA waiting at the end. There is much more going on here, but hopefully this is enough to convince you that you will not want to miss this one."*
~Emily Pennington on *Trey*

www.BOROUGHSPUBLISHINGGROUP.com

PUBLISHER'S NOTE: This is a work of fiction. Names, characters, places and incidents either are the product of the author's imagination or are used fictitiously. Any resemblance to actual events, locales, business establishments or persons, living or dead, is coincidental. Boroughs Publishing Group does not have any control over and does not assume responsibility for author or third-party websites, blogs or critiques or their content.

ISBN: 978-1-957295-18-3

*To my family for their unwavering support.*
*I love all of you to the moon and back.*

# SPENCER

# CHAPTER ONE
*Spence*

Someone was staring at him, but Spence didn't bother turning around. Instead, he continued his workout as if he were alone. The sun had begun to crest over the trees, its reflection shining across the lake giving life to its name: Fire Lake. He liked to get in his workout before the sun heated up the pseudo gym his team had created in the yard behind the house facing the water.

He delivered a mean uppercut to the punching bag they'd hung from one of the larger tree limbs and followed it up with a roundhouse kick that sent the bag flying back on its chain. On missions, he never knew when it would come down to hand-to-hand combat up close and personal. He had to be prepared.

Combining lethal damage in a minimal amount of time was key in the field, where his team was often outnumbered. He'd chosen a mixture of martial arts and Krav Maga to stay in shape and keep himself out of trouble when on missions. Having mastered a range of disciplines made him even deadlier: Jujitsu, Brazilian Jiu-Jitsu, Muay Thai, and Krav Maga made for a powerful arsenal.

His muscles flexed and burned with every move as he delivered blow after blow to the bag. Sure, it was brutal and aggressive, but his work required it. He wasn't dancing in a ring with some dude who had to follow rules. Ten times out of ten, he was on an op where he was confronted with a trained killer who wanted to make Spence the next notch on a belt. He made no excuses. He was what he was: a computer geek extraordinaire who was highly trained by the Navy SEALs to remove all obstacles through various methods.

Sounded a whole hell of a lot better than a trained killer with PTSD.

He caught himself before he went down that dark and dangerous path. Especially since he'd been enjoying showing off for his audience when his fucked-up brain decided to take him to the dark side. How was he supposed to enjoy this new life when he couldn't get his mind out of the past?

The snap was his only warning. A millisecond later, the limb broke, sending the bag, its chain, and the branch flying into the lake a few feet away.

*Shit.*

\*\*\*

*Rick*

Rick watched as Spence waded into the water to retrieve the punching bag and the tree limb. Rick had been standing on the deck spellbound, watching as the object of his desire beat the crap out of the bag. Spence was a bit shorter than the giants who lived at the lake house, but he lacked none of their muscle tone and capabilities and had a hell of a lot of finesse.

Watching him work out had been Rick's favorite pastime when he came to Fire Lake with his boss and friend, Roman, who was dating the former SEAL team leader, Brick. It seemed crazy when he looked back at all that had happened to get him here.

"You may want to back up a little, so he doesn't see you." Roman's voice came from behind him and almost made him jump.

"Don't you know better than to sneak up on someone?" Rick growled.

"I wasn't sneaking. You were so oblivious I could've been stomping for all you knew." Roman laughed. "I can see why."

Rick spun around and headed into the kitchen to finish making breakfast. This wasn't a conversation he wanted to have, and he chose to busy himself cooking something nutritious for the team, who eschewed his efforts. He added Ben, Gunner's nephew, to the new, more nutritious diet.

When he'd first arrived at the lake house over a year ago to help Roman while he was away from his Dallas head office of Furrow and Son's Investments, Rick had noted no one living here ate properly. Their nutrition consisted of fats, sugars, and salts. Even considering all of them were in optimal shape thanks to their training and work, time would still catch up with them.

The average age around the house, not including the kids, was forty-three. Eating like teenagers was a surefire way to ensure none of them would age well. They needed proper nutrition to keep them going through their missions. The heavy physical toll on their bodies made it more likely for them to fall prey to a slipup that could end one of their lives.

He couldn't allow that to happen.

Not on his watch.

Roman would be devastated if something were to happen to his lover. That was Rick's reasoning, and he would do everything he could to make sure Roman and Brick had a long, healthy life together.

"Why won't you admit you have a thing for Spence?" Roman asked as he refilled his coffee mug from an enormous machine, which was better suited to be manned by a trained barista. Julia, the team's admin, loved it, so *c'est la vie.*

"Because I don't," Rick muttered. He put a pot of water on the stove for their steel-cut oatmeal. He'd even brought organic wildflower honey from his favorite farmers' market. Fresh organic fruit would be next as he took out the cutting board and retrieved the melon, kiwi, strawberries, and apples from the crisper in the fridge.

"That's a lie," Roman called him on it. "I've known you all my life, bud."

"Yeah, the good, bad, and the ugly," Rick mumbled.

"What the hell? He's cooking again," Fletch yelled across the room as he stood at the bottom of the stairs.

"Yes, I am," Rick stated. Fletch was the most outspoken critic of Rick's healthy eating campaign. While the others surely agreed, they seemed fine with letting Fletch be the house spokesman. "You'll eat it and enjoy it, you redheaded behemoth."

Fletch grumbled and went out the French doors to the lake where Spence was wrangling with the wet punching bag. Rick carried on with slicing and dicing until he had a bowl full of mixed fruit goodness. When he turned, he found Roman still standing in front of the coffee machine.

"Even though we've been friends for far more years than I'd like to admit, we don't share *everything*."

"True enough," Roman admitted. "And you don't look a day over twenty-eight."

"One of the reasons we're still friends." Rick laughed.

"Okay. If you're not ready to discuss your obsession with Spence, how about the reason you've taken over cooking when we're here?"

"I want them to eat better."

"Because…?"

"I'm a nice person?"

Roman sighed. "I know Arthur died from heart disease."

"Yes, I'm aware." And Rick missed him every day.

"It's obvious you're compensating. Sure, you care so much about the team, especially one information specialist, but you're overdoing it with the healthy food."

Rick stopped and pointed his chopping knife at Roman. "Swear you won't tell them."

"What?"

He looked Roman straight in the eyes. "Swear it. No one needs to know about my past."

"I would never tell anyone about your past. I swear it. Totally your business. I'm sorry. I should'nt've brought it up."

Rick's heart beat wildly in his chest, but he'd accepted Roman's apology. There was no way he'd tell anybody how scared he was to lose the people he loved and cared about. "It's okay, but that part of my life stays between you and me. If they were to find out, they'd hate me more than they already do."

"They don't hate you."

*Now there's a good friend. Lie to my face to make me feel better.* "Yeah, right. I've accepted it." Sort of.

Roman looked like he wanted to argue the point, but sighed heavily and leaned against the counter.

"Now put the twelve-grain bread in the toaster, and I'll scramble the free-range egg whites." Rick knew his place in the household pecking order and used snark and indifference to protect himself. It'd been that way since he was a child. Why change now?

"Seriously, babe. Why is Rick cooking?" Brick asked as he joined them in the kitchen.

"Because he's a good person," Roman snapped.

"He means I'm a good dietician and can be useful," Rick clarified and shot Roman a glare.

"Yeah, dietician. Right," Roman mumbled, and Brick let it go.

After Rick got the food on the table, he intended to sit on the deck far away from the complaints without appearing to be rude.

More people arrived, and Rick did his best to carry on as the comments flew. "I need real food," "Why are you punishing us," and other comments of the like circled the kitchen. He finished Ben's breakfast and brought it to the youngster's spot at the table. The boy dug in without complaint.

Gunner asked, "You like that?"

Ben looked up innocently and said, "Yeah. Mommy made breakfast like this all the time."

Gunner gave Rick a weird look, making him feel self-conscious. He turned away and went back into the kitchen. Once he had everything prepared and on trays, he set them, along with the fresh-squeezed orange juice, on the kitchen table and walked away without looking at Spence.

Grabbing his laptop, he headed for the far end of the deck. At least Ben appreciated his efforts. He could live with that small victory.

Rick turned on his laptop to get the latest numbers on the company's investments and caught up on any emails he might've missed. He may be at the lake house, but work didn't end when they left the office. He saw a personal email waiting for him, which struck him as odd because only a handful of people knew his email address.

He opened it, expecting to see some advertising trying to sell him the latest and greatest, but quickly realized his mistake.

*Hello Rick.*

> *Did you honestly think you could leave? This isn't the type of arrangement you can walk away from. The old man's dead, and you may have changed your name, but we both know who and what you really are. Come back before I send out Spike to collect you from your new friends.*
> *You have seven days.*

*Simon*

As he stared at the screen, Rick's body shook uncontrollably. Fifteen years of freedom ended in one email. He knew what he had to do. He'd prepared for this day while praying it would never come.

"Are you okay?" Spence asked, making Rick jump and close the laptop. "Whoa. Easy, man. It's only me. What's wrong?"

Rick had to pull himself together and bury his fear. "What the hell are you doing scaring me like that?" He felt like shit for snapping at Spencer, but telling him the truth would be a surefire way of losing whatever friendship they may have built.

"I'm sorry. Didn't mean to," Spence said. "But you were upset before I said anything. What's going on?"

Spence was highly intelligent. Rick should've known he wouldn't get off so easily.

"Nothing."

"Right, and I'm as lethal as a butterfly."

"The *Papilio antimachus* is one of the most lethal butterflies in the world. They secrete poison hunters use on their arrows to take down prey. Even large animals drop dead of heart attacks when the arrow pierces them."

Spence didn't seem fooled by the obscure info dump. Maybe he already knew about the *antimachus* butterfly. Rick knew he was grasping at straws. Then he thought, given Spence's background and mad skills, maybe Spence could help him.

*No. I'm not dragging him into this.*

"Personal issues. We all have them." He shrugged and tried to appear nonchalant.

"Is there anything I can do to help?"

*Yes.* "No. I'll take care of it myself but thank you for the offer."

Instead of leaving, Spence sat in the chair a few feet away.

"You not eating?" Rick asked, feeling the rejection in his gut.

"I've already finished. The honey was a nice change-up."

He must've been sitting and staring at his screen longer than he thought for Spence to've had time to eat a complete meal. Rick blamed it on the shock of hearing from a man he'd hoped was dead.

Seven days wasn't long to put his escape plan into action. He had a lot of things to do, yet he couldn't pull himself away from sitting and talking with Spence.

"I'm surprised you noticed. Since my last visit, how many bags of barbeque chips have you gone through?"

"I don't know what you're talking about."

"Yeah, yeah. I brought you a healthier alternative to your deep-fried, salt-laden snack of choice. I placed the bags in the cupboard for you to try. If you like them, there's information on the bags on how to reorder."

Spence cocked his head. "Why would I have to order them when you can bring more when you come back?"

"I'm not always going to be around," Rick said without thinking. *Shit.* "I mean, I have a life outside of working for Roman." *Yeah, right.*

As Spence leaned forward, his eyes narrowed.

"How was your workout?" *Like Rick didn't know.*

"Good. I'm going to have to rehang the bag though," he said sheepishly. "I like training when it's quiet and cool."

"I know."

"Hmm?"

"I meant I know what you mean. It can get hot around here fast."

Spence rubbed the back of his neck before asking, "What are your plans today?"

"Sorting through some paperwork." *And trying to get everything in place before I'm forced to leave.*

"I was thinking of taking a boat ride. Wanna come?"

*Yes.* He did. But he knew better. "I'm sorry. I have work to complete for Roman."

"Oh, that's okay," Roman said as he came around the corner. "I'm giving you the day off. Go have fun."

Spence's eyes sparkled, and for a long moment, Rick contemplated refusing, but then he'd have to explain why to Roman. *Because my fucked-up past has come back to bite me in the ass* wasn't the answer he was prepared to share. And damnit, he wanted to go with Spence, and this was the last chance he'd have.

"Okay. When do we leave?"

# CHAPTER TWO
*Spence*

Spence suspected Rick was dealing with something seriously wrong and hoped he could get to the bottom of it while they were out on the water alone where Rick would have no place to run and hide. He'd been thinking about asking Rick out to dinner, but the look on his face this morning, when he didn't think Spence knew he was watching him work out—again—had him accelerating his plans. The look on Rick's face when Spence came up on him had him changing his tactics.

He recognized fear when he saw it.

When Rick mentioned he'd brought a healthier snack to replace Spence's barbeque chip addiction, it punched him straight in the heart. No one had gone out of their way for him except his team. The effort made him feel cared for. While the rest of the team grumbled and bitched about Rick's food, Spence knew he felt better and had more energy in the last couple of months since Rick had taken over cooking many of their meals and stocking the house with healthier options.

Ben, the four-year-old, had dug in because he said it was like his mother's cooking. And that was all the endorsement he needed: the food was made with love.

After Rick said he'd be right back and headed into the house with his laptop, Spence went to the dock to ready the boat.

Julia got to the dock before Rick and said, "Here you go. I've made you lunch for your boat ride." She handed him a large picnic basket.

"Thanks," he told her while reaching for the basket. "This'll come in handy." He hadn't thought of it, but having food would allow them to stay out longer.

She smiled but didn't return to the lake house. Instead, she stood there as if working up the courage to say what was on her mind.

"Anything else?"

She sucked in a deep breath and said in a rush, "Please be nice to Rick." His head jerked back. "He's a good person and has helped me out when I needed some advice. I know he's into you. Don't lead him on if you're not interested."

*Helped her?* "Are you okay?"

She smiled wide. "Yep."

"Great. Listen, I don't intend to hurt him. I'm hoping to get to know him better." Which was the truth. Sure, attraction went only so far, but he knew enough about relationships to know he needed more than lust for the glue that hung two people together.

"Okay. I hope I didn't offend you," she said.

"All's good. I appreciate your concern." He liked knowing other people were looking out for the guy.

She smiled and nodded before walking away. Spence stowed the basket under the console, and moments later, Rick came walking down the dock. His sandy blond hair was styled, and his hoodie and jeans were designer, along with his bright blue eyeglass frames that highlighted his dark blue eyes.

His outward appearance exuded confidence, but something in his eyes drew Spence in. His heart rate sped up the closer the man got.

Rick was the smallest guy in the house: roughly five-seven, nearly six inches shorter than Spence, who was the shortest man in the team by at least a half foot.

Rick was beautiful with pouty lips, high cheekbones, and a cleft chin covered in a day's worth of stubble. Usually, he was clean-shaven and wearing a suit, but seeing him in his casual clothes and unshaven did something to Spence's easy-to-rev libido.

"What are you staring at?" Rick asked as he neared with arms crossed and his usual snark in place.

"A handsome man headed my way," Spence answered without bothering to filter his words. He'd been holding back for the last six months, not wanting to mess things up. No more. He was ready to lay it all on the line starting today. Especially since he wanted to get to the bottom of what was going on in Rick's personal life. Scared wasn't a good look on anyone.

Rick's cheeks reddened at the compliment, making Spence feel ten feet tall. He held out his hand to help Rick aboard the small six-seater. His touch sparked Spence's body, as it always did, and he wondered if Rick had the same reaction.

Instead of acknowledging what Spence said, Rick asked, "Where are we headed?"

Once Rick was seated, Spence started the engine and untied them from the dock. "I wanted to share a special spot I've discovered."

"Okay. I'm intrigued."

"Good. Sit back and relax. I'll be your tour guide."

Rick gave him an odd smile before saying, "I'll try."

"That's all I can ask."

"You're easy to please." Rick grinned. At least he was smiling again.

"Remember that when I have you trekking through the bush." Bush may be an exaggeration, but Rick might consider it bushwhacking.

"Bush? I didn't agree to that," Rick said but didn't look overly upset.

"I know." Spence laughed. "That's why I waited until we cast off from the dock to tell you."

Rick shielded his eyes from the bright sun with his hand. "Always thinking ahead, aren't you?" Spence removed his sunglasses and handed them to Rick. "Thanks," he muttered.

"In my world, that's normal behavior, or disasters happen."

Rick's expression tightened. "You're reasonably safe on these missions, right?"

"As safe as could be in some situations."

"That's why training is so important."

"Yeah. That's why we train every day."

"Do you think you could teach me a self-defense move or two?" Rick asked without making eye contact.

Something was up. "Sure. We can start when we get back." This was the perfect chance to test the waters. "Is there someone specific you want to prepare for?"

"Nah. There's no particular reason, but it would be good to know if the need ever arises," Rick was quick to say. "I have a bit of work to do first when we get back. After I'm done would be great."

"We have a plan. Now sit back and enjoy the boat ride." Spence let it go for now. Rick's expression didn't lie, even if his words did.

Something had him worried, and Spence intended to find out who or what that was.

***

*Rick*

The endless blue sky glowed as they skipped across the water. A perfect day for a boat ride. But, even though he was mere feet away from the object of his desire, he couldn't shake the dread building inside of him.

Before reading that damned email, Rick would've given anything to be alone with the handsome, dark, and dangerous man. Spending time together without the rest of the team around sounded like heaven and would've been. Except...

How the hell had Simon found him? Rick had been careful to cover his tracks. It'd been a long time since he'd last seen that psycho. What the hell could he want?

"You don't look like you're relaxing," Spence said, bringing Rick out of his thoughts. He'd need to be more careful around him and the others, or else he'd give himself away.

"I'm not used to relaxing during the day. There's always work to get done."

"We'll have to change that," Spence replied. "You can't go around tied up in knots day after day. You, of all people, know that's unhealthy."

He did know that, and he agreed stress was a killer. But so was Simon. "I'll try harder."

Spence reached over and laid his big hand on Rick's shoulder. "If you need anything, you come to me. Even if it's only to talk. Understand?"

His dark eyes bore through him, and Rick felt naked. All he could manage was to nod in agreement. Damn, every cell in his body stood at attention, and he could feel his body leaning toward Spence. Luckily, he came to his senses before he found himself in the muscled man's arms.

How did Spence have this much power over him? Rick had been in control of his own life when he parted ways with Simon and fought for that strength and independence. But a look from Spence could bring him to his knees. And, unlike Simon, Spence didn't invoke terror. Quite the opposite.

When Spence looked away, Rick was able to refocus on the water. He sucked in a deep breath to clear his thoughts, only to fill his senses with Spence's unique scent. A combination of leather, pine trees, and freshwater. It was intoxicating, and he struggled to block its effects.

Now was the wrong time for this to be happening. Rick had seven days to run, but to where was the question. Maybe being alone was his fate. He should've known better than to form any attachments, and yet here he was on a boat ride with what could have been his biggest attachment of all.

His days with these people were numbered, but he didn't think he could pull himself away from whatever this was between him and Spence.

Was he selfish or stupid?

He'd find out in seven days.

# CHAPTER THREE

*Spence*

Spence maneuvered the boat closer to their stop, a midsize uninhabited island more than fifty minutes away from the lake house. It was heavily wooded, and from the squawking and chirping, wildlife was obviously abundant. Plus, this island held a surprise behind the walls of foliage.

"We're stopping here?" Rick asked while scanning the area. "Doesn't look like much."

"Everyone knows you shouldn't judge a book by its cover."

Rick lowered his head before saying, "You're right."

Spence jumped off the boat onto the shore and pulled the boat close so Rick could easily join him, and then he tied the rope to a nearby cedar tree.

"Ready to get your feet wet?" Spence asked as he held out his hand.

Rick looked down at his shoes. "These are designer."

Spence smiled wide. Rick's shield was back in place, but Spence knew he could draw the real Rick out again. "Expensive, I bet. Then they should be comfortable for walking. Good choice." He enjoyed goading the typically aloof man to unearth another spark of emotion. A fire burned inside Rick, but he kept it under lock and key.

"That's not what I meant."

Spence didn't budge. He'd wait as long as it took for Rick to trust him because that was what this was really about.

After a few more scans of the tree line, Rick nodded and took hold of Spence's hand. That same zing of awareness raced down his arm, causing the short black hairs to rise. He'd never get tired of that feeling.

"Okay, show me what's so impressive about this place," Rick mumbled as he gained his balance.

"Follow me." Spence winked before turning and heading straight into the brush.

He didn't take off at his usual pace, which would've left Rick to fend for himself. He went slow and chose the easiest terrain to cross. He turned to check on Rick every few feet, whose expression said it all. Spence was in for hell when they stopped, which made him smile all the more.

"How are you doing back there? Not too tough for ya?"

"I can keep up if that's what you're asking," Rick shot back.

"Good, good. So, what did you like to do as a kid?" Spence figured he had to start somewhere to unravel the tight ball Rick had wound himself into. "I was always running the streets. Drove my mom nuts."

When Rick didn't answer, Spence went at it differently. "I bet you were the kinda kid who had to be forced to go outside."

"There is nothing wrong with being inside your own space, but I'll have you know me and my dad lived on Canyon Lake, northeast of San Antonio. I grew up fishing and hiking almost daily."

Spence had to wonder what changed in Rick's life to stop him from being who he was raised to be. It was obvious by his unsure steps he hadn't been hiking in a hell of a long time.

"Really? Did you move away or go to school in a city?"

Rick's face darkened. "You can say that." Before Spence could continue his questioning, Rick asked, "Did you go to college or straight into the Navy?"

He had been well-trained in the art of questioning captives as well as having a heavy dose of common sense and street smarts. He appreciated having the table turned. Good tactic. "Straight into the Navy. Like my dad before me, and his dad."

"So, serving is a sort of family tradition?"

"In my family, yeah. There's been a Moretti involved in some part of the military since World War One. Unfortunately, in my lifetime, I've lost an aunt, who served in the Gulf in 1991, and we lost a cousin in 2008 from a pipe bomb explosion in Iraq."

"Honorable and tragic," Rick said. "Saying thank you to you and your family for their service sounds hollow compared to your family's sacrifices."

"It's still appreciated." Any day someone thanked a vet and remembered their sacrifices was a good day. He pulled the neck of his t-shirt to one side to reveal one of his many tattoos. This one was the roman numerals XXVI. "My cousin was only twenty-six."

"So young." Rick's tone and expression were a sharp departure from his usual demeanor, and Spence caught a glimpse of the real man underneath for the first time. Those blue eyes, full of sadness, were locked on his own, and Rick's voice shook slightly before he cleared it with a cough. "It's a lot to give up to keep me and society safe."

Spence felt those words. He couldn't explain it. Of course, he'd heard them before, and he always appreciated each person for saying them. However, this time it hit home harder than before. His heart rate sped up while his stomach squeezed.

"Thanks for, ah, saying so." Spence's voice broke.

Long moments passed, and neither looked away. Lord knew how long they stood there like that, but the cry of a passing heron broke the spell.

"So, um… You were going to show me something," Rick said while blinking a few times before looking the other way.

"Yeah. Though I'd prefer to stay here and stare at you."

"You don't even know me," Rick countered.

"I know you're not the crusty-assed person you pretend to be. I know the real you is in there, and it comes out when you're caring for people. You can't dim that light. I've seen it."

Rick looked nervous. "Yeah, yeah, I'm a real saint. Let's get on with this tour from hell."

Spence couldn't help his smile. He had expected nothing less. "It's not far now." He grinned and turned around then headed farther into the island's center.

He could hear Rick following behind him by the thud of his feet and the movement of the brush around him. He'd be easy to find if they somehow got split up.

"Okay, first lesson. If you're trying to hide, you need to be aware of your noise. Someone would find you without much effort with all the banging and carrying on you're making."

Rick didn't respond, but almost instantly, there was a reduction in his noise level, which led Spence to surmise a person was worrying the guy, and that person was up to no good.

The breeze riffled through the thinning trees closer to their destination. Instead of walking the last few steps himself, Spence held back the lower limbs of the trees and motioned for Rick to go ahead of them. He looked unsure. "I would never do anything to cause you harm."

With a slight nod, Rick passed Spence and gasped. No matter what the mercurial man had expected, he liked what he saw.

When Spence followed through the tree line, he found Rick standing a couple of feet ahead, scanning the area.

"How did you find this?"

"Exploring."

"Do you come here often?"

"As often as possible."

"It's beautiful."

"Agreed."

Spence looked around at the scene more reminiscent of fantasy than reality. The clearing was covered in colorful flowers and had a small pond on the far end. Rocks mixed with grassy patches formed a mosaic that could be created only by mother nature. Mockingbirds flew across the clearing to their nests high up in the surrounding oak trees, and a small beaver mound sat along the pond's edges, redirecting the flow of water from one of the two streams.

The sun glowed high above them, but it couldn't outshine the smile on Rick's face as he took in his surroundings. "It's like a picture. Too beautiful to be real. Like one of those fairy fantasy scenes they put in movies."

*Exactly.* "I'm glad you like it," Spence said. "Would you like to explore farther in?"

Rick spun around and pretty much shouted, "Yeah." Spence could feel the lump he carried around in his stomach become lighter. "Have you ever seen anyone else out here?"

Spence took hold of Rick's hand and led him to the pond. Rick didn't fight him, so he took it as a win. "No. I've been out here a bunch of times and have never seen any trace of other people visiting this spot."

"A secret," Rick said softly. "I read a story about a garden like this when I was a kid. It'd been shut away and hidden."

"Did you enjoy the book?"

"Yes. When I was a kid, I'd dream of secret spaces where no one could find me."

That set off alarms in Spence's mind. He could think of many reasons a child would want to hide away. He logged that thought. Pieces of the puzzle were being laid out, but there was no discernable pattern yet.

"Well, if you want, you can consider this place your secret hideaway. The guys don't know about it. I kept it to myself." He liked to come out here to think when so many of his missions refused to give him peace.

"You haven't told anyone, but you brought me here." Rick squinted as he asked, "Why?"

"Because I want to share it with only you." Spence wanted to share more with the man if he'd let him.

Rick's expression hadn't changed. It seemed like he was trying to read Spence's truthfulness. And that was all right. He liked being the center of Rick's attention, and remained still. Waiting.

Rick threw out his arm and pointed at Spence. "What's your game?"

"I'm not playing a game. I want to get to know you, if you let me."

Rick's head tilted, making Spence want to pull him into his arms, but he figured too much too soon.

"What if you don't like what you find?"

"Everyone has a past. The glimpses I've had underneath all your well-constructed armor have shown me the caring, loyal, protective person you are. Whatever you're worried about can be dealt with." Before Rick had a chance to argue, Spence carried on. "How about I go back to the boat and grab our lunch. If you want me to take you back to the lake house, I will."

"And you'll give up on this?"

"Hell no. I'll come up with a new plan."

Even though he was sure Rick fought it, a grin broke out across his face. He shook his head and pointed to the way they'd come. "Go get the food, weirdo."

"Yesss," Spence hissed before turning and taking off at a jog. "Be right back."

\*\*\*

*Rick*

*What the hell am I doing?*

He should be preparing to get the hell out of Dodge, not picnicking. Clearly, he had lost his damn mind. Simon gave him seven days, and Rick couldn't waste them. Yet here he was, standing on an island in the middle of a lake, staring at flowers and lusting after a delicious former Navy SEAL.

A couple of hours ago, he would've given his right nut to spend time with Spence. Now he was debating whether to have the guy take him back to the lake house so he could pack and get back to Dallas or stay and enjoy the little time he'd have with a guy who'd crept under his skin before he could stop him.

The rustle of grass and splash of water had Rick turning back to the pond. The beaver residents had come out of their mud-and-stick mound to take a leisurely swim around the pond. It all seemed so peaceful and *right*. He understood the draw for a man like Spence, who, given his profession, surely hadn't seen much peace in his life.

Rick remembered a time when he had no peace, home, money, friends, or family. What would he have given to find a place like this. He'd been lucky and found a place where he belonged the day he'd met Arthur. But that'd been a lifetime ago.

"Ready?"

Rick spun around with his fists at the ready to fight off, fight off... He'd been lost in his thoughts and acted on instinct.

"It's me," Spence said as he backed up several feet, placed the basket on the ground, and held his hands out to his sides.

Adrenaline pumped through Rick's veins as he fought to lower his fists. "You scared the hell out of me. Make a goddamn noise next time, would ya?"

There was no anger on Spence's face, only concern, which made Rick feel like an asshole. The email had him spooked. And just now, he'd given away too much. He shook out his arms and looked away.

"Sorry," Spence mumbled as he lowered his hands and approached him. "Are you all right?"

"A little jumpy from being in a new place, I guess." A bullshit answer, and Spence wasn't buying it.

"How about we set up lunch so you can relax a little?"

"Sounds good." Rick needed to sit down. With the adrenaline slipping away and Simon's return looming, he needed to regroup or pass out. It'd been a stressful morning.

Spence picked the basket up and took hold of Rick's hand before leading him to a shady patch under a tree near the pond. He spread out the blanket on the grass and motioned for Rick to join him. Spence ran his palm down Rick's face, then his long, strong fingers started rubbing his temples.

"Water?" Spence asked as he dropped his hands. Rick still felt the rough pads soothing his anxiety as he stared at the bottle Spence held out to him.

"Thanks." Rick twisted the cap and raised the shaking bottle to his lips, which he was sure Spence saw.

He had to get a handle on himself.

Everything was spiraling out of control.

# CHAPTER FOUR
*Spence*

Something was seriously wrong. Rick had jumped at least a foot off the ground when Spence had approached with the picnic basket. That was the behavior of a terrorized person who'd been through some sort of hell. He would know. There were dark fears plaguing the man who maintained control to within an inch of his life. Oh yeah, there was so much more to him than being Roman's assistant. Spence figured that was a good place to start to unravel the truth. Safe ground to cover that might calm Rick while Spence unearthed some salient facts.

"You like working for Roman?" Spence asked as he laid out plates and utensils before spreading out the food Julia had packed. There was a large cheese and meat tray, along with rolls, butter over ice, condiments, and for dessert, everyone's favorite: chocolate chip cookies.

Julia was a godsend. She kept LH Investigations running with efficiency and ensured everything was up to date while she herded the team, organized their lives, and kept their records straight. She was entrusted with everyone's personal information and all cases they took on. She was a wizard with numbers, and Rick had helped her set up the accounting programs to help make sure the numbers added up.

"I love working for Roman. I'm lucky to have him as my boss and friend." Rick's face lost some of its stress as Spence had hoped.

"Sounds the same as the way I view Brick. He's the leader. He's earned the right and our respect. But he's also my friend."

"Exactly," Rick replied before reaching for a roll.

"We've been following Brick for a lotta years, and he's never steered us wrong. How long have you known Roman?" he asked as he constructed a sandwich.

"Since I was fourteen," Rick answered. "We became friends playing a video game online. We didn't meet in person until many years later."

Rick followed suit and made himself a sandwich with extra cheese and a healthy dose of mustard. His hands were still shaking, though considerably less. Spence was tuned into his every move.

"What game did you guys play?"

"The Realm, an RPG. I know what you're thinking, geeky role-playing games, but it was fun and new tech at the time I used to love escaping into." He looked away and took a bite of his sandwich.

There was that word again, escape.

"I wouldn't say geek. I'll admit to being on a quest or two. Besides, I spend a lot of my time on my laptop. No judgment here."

"Yeah, but you're a Navy SEALs hacker. That's a bit more serious than Wizard Felcor of Tenor."

"When I was younger, I traveled through the worlds of D and D on many a quest. So don't be hard on yourself."

Rick's smile was instant, and Spence thought he'd do almost anything to see that smile every day. They both tucked into their lunch and ate in companionable silence. The air was still, and the only sounds came from the beavers splashing in the pond. This serenity was why Spence loved this place as much as he did. A man could think out here or be quiet while the world spun outside his private sanctuary.

Spence's focus turned to the sun highlighting Rick's blond hair, making each strand appear golden. He itched to touch it to feel if it was as soft as it looked. What a sap. He remembered teasing Shaw about getting soft, and here he was doing the same damn thing.

A few birds came to land near them, and Rick broke off a couple of pieces from his bun to throw to them. It wasn't long before their fellow feathered friends joined the first two, hoping to score a free lunch.

Spence held out a second bun to Rick who ate his sandwich while feeding the birds. For a few moments, Rick's expression relaxed and he seemed in the moment, until he realized he was being watched.

"Why are you staring at me?"

"Because you're really hot when you're happy."

"Really hot? Have you lost your mind?"

"No. You're handsome all the time, but you go off the charts when you smile."

"You need your eyes checked." Rick's dismissal surprised Spence. Surely, the guy had compliments hitting him all the time.

"Had them checked last month, Twenty-ten. Better than perfect. I see just fine," Spence said, but he changed the subject, not wanting to belabor the point. "Did you live in Canyon Lake most of your life?"

"Until I was fifteen."

Spence waited for more, but Rick went back to eating his sandwich. This getting to know each other was going to be like pulling hen's teeth.

"As a military brat, I've lived all over the world. It went with the territory. When I was old enough, I joined the Navy and continued the tradition."

"Were you lonely moving around so much?"

"At times I felt isolated. I'd make new friends, and then we were moving again a year or two later. It wasn't easy, and I spent a fair amount of time alone, but I was proud of my family."

"That had to be hard." By the compassion coming off Rick in waves, Spence guessed he knew something about loneliness.

"Yeah, it had its challenges. Where did you and your dad move after Canyon Lake?"

"Chicago."

"Wow, that had to be a shock. Where was your mom?" He hadn't mentioned her once.

"She took off when I was young."

"Ah, shit. I'm sorry, man. I didn't mean to drag up past pain." What an asshole move. He hadn't thought that one out.

Rick reached over and placed his hand on top of Spence's. "It's okay. From what I've learned, I had a much better life without her being around, at least until...."

"Until?"

Rick seemed to snap out of it, and Spence watched as Rick's eyes shuttered, and those walls were thrown back up. "Nothing. Everything was wonderful."

*Right.*

"We should be getting back," Rick said as he began gathering the leftover food into the basket.

Spence knew their time together was over, but he couldn't help trying for a few more minutes. "We can leave the basket here and come back for it. There's one more place on the island I want to show you."

Rick looked hesitant, but then nodded. The man was a mystery, and Spence hadn't dug much further into him other than performing a perfunctory check when Roman was being stalked. Then once Spence met Rick and got to know him, it felt like a betrayal of trust doing a more in-depth look around into his past without a legitimate reason.

But that didn't mean he wasn't going to let Rick keep himself hidden.

\*\*\*

*Rick*

He wished this adventure didn't have to end, but facts were facts. Rick would have to leave for Dallas as soon as possible, and no amount of wishing or dreaming could change that. He should've known better than to have let his guard down, especially since his past was now very much in the present, which meant he had to leave. Immediately.

"It's not far now," Spence said as his hold on Rick's hand tightened. "I'm glad you came out here with me today."

Rick couldn't lie. "So am I."

Even with the guillotine prepped and the blade hanging high above his neck, he wanted to steal a few more moments with Spence. He'd wanted this, them alone, getting to know each other, since the day they met. There was no harm in admitting it, especially since there was nothing he could do about it now. These few hours would have to hold him for a lifetime. A special memory he could pull out and enjoy. But it could never be anything more.

They were climbing higher, and soon the trees cleared, and the view before him was gloriously panoramic. He was mesmerized and had barely registered they'd stopped walking. The sun, high in the sky, was occasionally obscured by giant cotton-ball clouds. The lake was calm and spread out in all directions, dotted by more islands, large and small.

Boats left their wake trails crisscrossing the water's surface, adding to the picturesque aspect. This was one of those instances where a photo could never do this scene justice. In this moment, Rick felt lucky. Spence was sharing this with him.

"You like?"

How could he put into words how this place made him feel? "It's stunning."

"We could sit if you want to stay for a while," Spence suggested as he pointed to his right. "There's a rock over here."

Rick knew he had to say no and get back to the lake house, but when he opened his mouth, "Sure," was what came out.

Spence's appealing smile lifted Rick's spirits, causing him to smile back and allow himself to be led over to the rock to have a seat. Rick wasn't sure how long they sat hand-in-hand, watching the boats from their perch.

A large part of him wanted time to stop so he could stay here like this forever. However, reality required he get back to the lake house and get back to Dallas. He turned to face Spence to tell him it was time to go, but was struck mute by the look on Spence's face: pure happiness. The guy was blissed out.

Rick was filled with so many emotions he was surprised his nervous system didn't short out. He was lost in the tumble and couldn't help but lean closer to Spence's biteable lips.

One moment they were staring at each other and then the next they were locked in a deep kiss, drinking each other in as if they were starving. It'd been a long time since Rick had allowed himself to lose control and act on his emotions. Even knowing this couldn't lead to anything, and dreading what his future held, he allowed himself to fall under Spence's spell.

His lips were as soft as they looked and his tongue mastered Rick's mouth. Excitement and need fought for supremacy as he dove deeper into the wonderous feeling of being in this man's arms. Spence's muscled body flexed, allowing Rick to explore that broad tattooed chest.

Over the past year, he'd dreamt about being in this exact position so many times, he was having a hard time believing it was true.

"Am I dreaming?"

"If you are, so am I. I'll clock anyone who tries to wake us up."

This was crazy. Irresponsible. Divine.

Spence's calloused hands slid under Rick's shirt, piling on another layer of sensation to his overstimulated body. Somehow, he ended up with his legs around Spence's waist, rubbing the growing bulge in his pants against those washboard abs he'd admired for so long from afar.

He was out of control and in no hurry to rein himself in until Spence's phone rang. Each chime knocked more and more sense into Rick and made him acutely aware of what he was doing.

He wanted Spence with every fiber of his being, no matter how hard he fought it. But he was leaving. For good. It wouldn't be fair to this decent, honorable man if they started something, and Rick took off.

He had to leave or Simon would come after him, putting everyone around him in danger. Simon preferred to let his gun do his talking and his henchmen do his dirty work without giving one shit about those caught in the crossfire.

Rick pulled away, and Spence didn't stop him, but he hadn't reached for his phone.

"Aren't you going to answer that?"

"Wasn't planning on it."

"It could be important. We should be going back anyway."

Spence nodded slowly. "Okay. I'll take you back."

He pulled his phone out and answered it. "Yeah."

Rick took the opportunity to put some distance between them and wrapped his arms around his suddenly chilled body. It seemed his fate was to never be free to live on his terms.

No matter how long he tried to stay hidden, Simon would always find him.

There was no way he'd get his friends involved in this.

Rick doubted he could handle seeing the look of disgust and disappointment on Spence's face if he ever found out the truth.

No. Rick had to leave.

There was no other choice.

# CHAPTER FIVE

*Spence*

"How was your boat ride?" Brick asked as he joined Spence, who was repairing the back porch before they installed a roof and enclosed it with screens. The bugs out here were murder.

"Fine." Spence was still trying to figure out what was going on with Rick. One moment he was all over him, and the next, he shut down. Completely. It didn't help Spence couldn't get the feeling of Rick's touch, his wet, delicious mouth, and his grinding hips off his mind.

Brick picked up a hammer, and Spence could tell the boss wanted to talk to him about something. He didn't have the patience to deal with waiting.

"What's up?"

"We have a mission out on the East Coast, New York. We leave tomorrow morning."

"What is it?"

"We've been hired to find a missing person. The girl is sixteen and was last seen nine days ago. The parents are television personalities and have called us in because the police are running out of leads."

"Who's going?"

"You, Gunner, and Fletch. I've left the brief on your laptop. Julia will be taking care of Ben. He and Sammy will be having a sleepover."

"What aren't you saying?"

Brick looked him straight in the eyes. "The maternal grandfather is Commander Rask."

Spence's alarm bells started banging at the name of a man who'd made it his mission to destroy Spence's Navy SEALs career. The only thing that'd saved him was the higher-ups belief in Spence, and Brick going to bat for him. If Rask'd had his way, Spence would've been out on his ass or stuck rotting in a brig somewhere. His only crime was sleeping with Rask's son, Jacob, a Navy ensign at the time.

The bastard claimed that Spence had used his influence to turn Jacob gay. As it turned out, Jacob went on to fuck his way through most of the available men on base. Rask retired early and still held a grudge against Spence.

"If you don't want to take this on, I can send Shaw in your place," Brick offered. "It's not a problem."

Spence didn't need time to think about it. "I'm in. We're the best hope of finding her. They'll need me."

"I was hoping you'd say that."

"I'll complete an initial assessment before we leave."

"Good. We'll meet at five hundred hours to go over what you've found," Brick agreed before changing his tone. "Things not work out as you'd hoped with Rick?"

"Something's upsetting him, and I don't know. He's hiding some deep...whatever. I'm not sure what it is, but he's spooked."

Brick tilted his head. "You haven't dug into his past?"

"Only as far as confirming he wasn't the person attacking Roman."

"Why are you holding back?"

"I want Rick to trust me enough to tell me about his past. It wouldn't feel right any other way."

Brick was quiet, and Spence knew he was considering his next words.

"Are you sure about him? He's difficult."

Spence understood the boss's concern, but it rubbed him wrong. "Rick is an amazing person if people would take the damn time to get to know him. Julia goes to him for advice, and he's helped her every time she's asked. I know everyone groans about the food he brings into this house, but he does it for the benefits it gives each of us. Remember when Kyle was healing? Rick made sure he had extra vitamins and proteins to help his recovery.

"He's selfless and he's devoted to Roman, your lover. Rick's built up defenses to deal with the world, but he's loyal and intelligent, caring and attuned to others' needs. Who else would take the daily for cooking us to make healthy meals? If that's what you consider difficult, I'm good with that. Maybe this world would be better off led by those who are *difficult*."

Brick pulled back as if he'd been sucker-punched. "I'm sorry, man. I didn't stop to think."

"Well, you're not alone in that. We've all been guilty of not seeing him for who he is. I'll go get started on the Rask family."

\*\*\*

*Rick*

Rick looked down at his phone in disbelief. How could there be no outbound flights to Dallas until tomorrow? He understood most airplanes were grounded due to a severe storm front moving in from the east, but getting away from Simon was a strong motivator and fucked with his logic.

*Maybe I should take my rental car home or leave everything in Dallas behind and hit the road from Marshall.* Rick glanced over at the small, black canvas bag packed inside his luggage. His bug-out bag. He'd kept one close all these years, and now he was thankful for the habit.

Inside was cash, a picture, and a gold chain. Cash, for obvious reasons, a picture of Arthur, and the only thing he had left of his father. There were enough clothes for three days and bank cards to accounts not under his current name. Money he'd hidden away long ago.

He'd hoped never to be forced to use the bag, but given the position he now found himself in, it was necessary. Fifteen years in this life he'd carefully created down the tubes with a couple strokes of a keyboard.

"Hey."

He jumped out of his chair and let loose an extremely unmanly squeal.

"It's me," Roman said as he held his hands up. "It's okay."

"You scared the hell out of me. Don't you know how to knock?" Rick's fear was driving his words. He felt bad the moment they left his mouth.

Roman's entire body went on alert. Rick could tell. He'd seen it happen before. His friend was analyzing his every move and word. Searching for any little bit of information so he could puzzle out Rick's behavior.

"So, are we going to play the game where you say nothing's wrong, and I have to pester you all day until you break, or can we cut to the chase, and you simply tell me what's going on?" Normally that would've made Rick laugh, but all the joy had been sucked out of him after receiving Simon's email.

"Nothing's wrong," he said eventually. "I have a few things to take care of back home, and I can't get a flight. You surprised me when you barged in."

"Okay, option one it is," Roman said, not fazed in the least by his attitude. "Did something happen with Spence when you two were out? Was he an asshole?" Roman went straight for the jugular. "If he did anything, I'll—"

"No, dad. He was a complete gentleman. Geesh. Spencer was his usual amazing self. He showed me a beautiful place that felt like it could be part of heaven, if there's such a thing. I'm the idiot who ruined the day by wanting to come back early. It has nothing to do with him. I simply need to go." It was starting to hit home how much he cared for Spence.

"I know how into him you are, and you had him all to yourself, but whatever is bothering you made you upset enough to ruin what you've wanted since laying eyes on him. Therefore, whatever it is you're not telling me has to be catastrophic for you to've blown him off."

"Quit trying to play detective. L. H. Investigations uses their talents to help the outside world, not me."

"I wouldn't be picking your lies apart if you'd 'fess up to what's going on," Roman argued. "You said help. Do you need help?"

Rick huffed and walked over to his waiting luggage he'd left open on the bed. Throwing a few shirts in, he bought some time to think of a way to get Roman off the scent. He couldn't tell his best friend the truth. Roman would rouse the team into action, putting them in danger. Simon was a killer.

Rick had seen it firsthand. It was one of his early lessons.

"Can't I have my own life away from here and you?" Rick growled the harsh words out though they gutted him.

Roman looked shocked as if Rick had told him to fuck off. "Of course, you can. I never said you couldn't."

"Then this is that time. I'm leaving to take care of some personal business."

His friend didn't look convinced, but thankfully Roman didn't push him further. "Okay, but if you need anything, you know you can come to me, right?"

Rick couldn't help but soften no matter how much he wanted to protect Roman and all the people in this house. He took a step forward. "Always." He had to close his eyes to prevent the tears from falling, and when he opened them again, Roman was gone.

His heart broke. Those could be his final words with Roman.

The only true friend he'd ever had.

# CHAPTER SIX

*Spence*

Commander Rask was a cold-hearted bastard. Fact, not opinion. But he could look past the POS when it came to the man's missing granddaughter, Ellen. The girl had nothing to do with Rask's bigotry. He wouldn't paint her with the same brush as her awful grandfather. Spence decided to treat this as he would any other case, starting with digging into all the players: Elise and Tom Hammon, Ellen's parents, their manager, Rask and each of his three wives, two former, one current, Jacob, and every person on the payroll of the morning show the parents hosted on a local television in New Rochelle, New York, a Westchester County suburb of New York City.

Both parents brought in hefty salaries supporting their lifestyle as minor celebrities. Each also held lucrative endorsement deals and sponsorships. By the looks of their flight history, they were away a lot of the year, making him wonder who raised Ellen. There wasn't a nanny listed as currently working for the family, but when he went deeper, he found that a nanny had been let go when Ellen had turned fourteen.

Spence began his mental checklist of unanswered questions, starting with: who stays with her when her parents are out of town?

Their house staff consisted of a cook, a maid, and a driver. He ran workups on each, finding a few interesting facts about their pasts. The driver was a convicted felon, and the cook and the maid were a mother-daughter team, having worked for the Hammons for decades.

They'd be a great source of information on the goings-on around the house.

*Why did they hire a felon as their driver? Did they know?*

Spence also found information suggesting Tom Hammon had an affair early on in their marriage, but the couple remained together. There were also rumors circulating about a possible love child from that affair. Spence would have to investigate the mistress and resulting child, who would now be eighteen years old.

As for Commander Rask, his exemplary military career was well documented, but there was precious little when it came to what Rask had done after retirement. He'd returned to his hometown in Kentucky with his third wife and essentially disappeared, as if he intentionally went off-grid. There were the usual federal tax returns but save that, not much came up.

Spence didn't buy it. A man like Rask didn't simply retire and do nothing but mow his lawn. It wasn't how he or any of his ilk were wired after a lifetime spent in the Navy. It didn't track. Spence would have to make a few calls.

As for Jacob, he did his time in the Navy and didn't re-up when his tour was over. He was currently living in Malibu, California working as a chef. Jacob was the product of Rask's first marriage, while his daughter, Elise, was from his second. Ellen was the only grandchild of the former commander.

As for the cast and crew of the Morning Show, they turned out to be a motley crew of individuals. A former NYC police officer ran security, a producer with a gambling problem, a meteorologist with several disturbing the peace charges, and a cameraman who spent his free time chasing UFOs and government conspiracies. And that was only scratching the surface.

It would take more time to go through each of them, but he concentrated his efforts on family for now. When someone goes missing, typically someone in the family knows more than they're saying.

According to the police report, Ellen had left for school as she usually did at eight in the morning, but never made it inside the school and was never seen again. Spence found it hard to believe. In today's society, it was almost impossible to go unseen. Before deciding, he'd have to look at the security footage at home, in the area, and at the school.

"You're already plugging away at our new case?" Gunner asked as he joined Spence on the back deck.

"Yeah. It's an interesting bunch, that's for sure."

"Rask of all people. What the hell are the odds of that?"

"Somewhere between the fuck too soon and burning in hell." There was no love lost between the team and Rask.

Gunner laughed, making Spence smile for the first time since leaving Rick's side.

"I feel for you, buddy. That shit's unbelievable. He was like a dog with a bone when it came to you."

"Thanks. With any luck, we won't have to cross paths often." Spence knew it was wishful thinking considering the missing girl was his granddaughter. "How's Ben settling in?"

"As good as can be expected without his mom."

"I'm so sorry about your sister, man. She was a good lady." The entire team had known Gunner's sister, and her death came as quite a shock.

"Yeah, she was. I miss her. It's weird because we hardly saw each other during my years SEAL years, but I could call her up at the drop of a hat, and she'd have time for me. She always had time to talk to me about everything going on."

Spence didn't know what to say, so he nodded as Gunner carried on.

"Life is so fucked up. I spent years saving others, and yet she died. How's that fair? Where's the karma in that shit?"

"Buddy, I wish I had the answer. Life sucks, and the only way to move forward is by being thankful for what you still have in Ben.

I'm sure his mom would be proud of how far you guys have come. Ben is happy and healthy. Sometimes that's all you can ask."

Gunner smiled. "I hope she is watching over him."

"Hell, he's in a house full of Navy SEALs. He's the safest kid on the planet."

That made his friend laugh, which was what Spence had intended. Gunner was a good man dealt a shitty hand. His family disowned him when he came out. Only his sister stood by his side through it all. Gunner had talked about his family a few times before, and they sounded like a bunch of typical hypocrites. Do what I say, not what I do types. His father had been having affairs for years, yet his mother stayed with the cheating ass "for better or worse." Adultery was more acceptable than being gay. One you could control. The other—not at all. Totally fucked-up thinking.

Before he and Gunner had a chance to continue their conversation, Roman and Brick walked out the garden doors and approached them. Spence went on alert as both men looked worried.

"We need to talk about Rick."

***

*Rick*

Rick was running, but he couldn't get away. His legs ached along with his lungs. How long had he been like this? Where was he, and what was he running from? Questions swirled through his mind, but he never stopped running.

He dared to look back and wished he hadn't. A beast with red, glowing eyes gained on him as his strength was waning. He looked down at his right hand to find he was carrying his bugout bag.

"Run, little street rat, run." Simon's voice was unmistakable as his words assaulted Rick from behind, cutting into his flesh, and still, he ran.

He'd never surrender. He'd choose death first. He felt something cold and heavy in his left hand and wasn't surprised to find a knife. This was how he'd get his freedom. This was the only way. As he lifted the knife to his chest, another voice broke through the darkness.

Spence.

"I'm here."

The beast disappeared, and so did Rick's bag and knife. He was alone but no longer afraid.

Rick woke from his nightmare as a storm raged outside the lake house. This weather was why he couldn't get a flight out tonight. The rain pelted the windows as the trees bent under the strength of the wind. Lightning flashed across the sky, followed by thunder so loud he swore it shook the house.

Using his thumb, he ghosted over the old scars on the inside of his thigh. A roadmap left over from a time when his depression and pain became too much for him to bear. Some of the scars were thick and bumpy, while others were merely a faint line. Memories he'd sooner forget assailed him, and he knew he wouldn't be getting any more sleep tonight.

He could hear footsteps moving around downstairs and was sure if they had to head to the new storm shelter the guys had built, they'd tell him. Rick glanced over at his packed bags, ready to go first thing in the morning, even if he had to drive his rental car to Dallas. The longer he waited, the more likely Simon would come here looking for him. Rick refused to allow that to happen to these people.

It wasn't as if he could call the team members his friends, except maybe Spence, but the rest of their team would gladly see him gone. He could admit he may have gone overboard on the healthy eating, and Roman may have been right when he said it was due to Arthur's death.

Rick thought he couldn't go on when he'd lost Arthur to heart disease and since seeing how these guys ate, he was forcing the entire house to eat a certain way because of his fear. No wonder they wanted him to stop cooking for them.

Well, they got their wish. They could fill the cupboards with fat-laden, processed food and salty snacks to their hearts' desire. However, he'd taken the time to make a list of foods and a menu for Ben he'd left for Gunner. The big guy wanted to do right by his nephew, and Rick knew that feeding the kid properly was something Gunner was concerned about.

As for Spence, he'd move on. It wasn't as if they were in a relationship or anything, even though the thought of Spence being with someone else made him nauseous. If he were being truthful with himself, he'd admit to lusting after the man from the first moment he laid eyes on him. In the course of the year, he'd known Spence, he'd grown to respect him for his work ethic and he admired his dedication to helping others.

Someone would come along and steal his heart. Unfortunately, it couldn't be Rick, no matter how much he wanted it to be.

*** 

The next morning Rick took a last look at the room he'd been staying in at the lake house. A single bed, a desk, a chair, dated wallpaper covering everything, and the worn wooden planks that squeaked no matter how softly he walked. It was perfect, and he would miss it.

The storm had passed during the night, and flights were again taking to the air. He'd be back in Dallas before lunch and out again before nightfall. To where, Rick wasn't entirely sure. He knew that the farther away from these people he went, the better. He doubted Simon would ever stop looking for him.

He sucked in a deep, fortifying breath, picked up his bag and coat, and opened the bedroom door. The house was as quiet as he'd hoped to make his clean getaway. He didn't expect anyone to be up at four-thirty in the morning. Slowly he inched his way down the hallway and to the stairs. He was halfway down when he realized he wasn't going to skulk out as he'd hoped.

"Good morning. I see you're up bright and early. Can I interest you in a cup of coffee?" Roman spoke as if it was a normal breakfast hour, especially when every team member and the sheriff stood facing him with their arms crossed, even Shaw, who technically didn't live at the lake house. *Well shit.*

"What's going on?" Like he didn't know.

Roman stepped away from Brick's side to stand in front of Rick. "The time for running is over, my friend. You didn't honestly think I bought all that private life bullshit? Since we were teenagers, we've shared everything, and no amount of pushing will make me move. You're not going out to face Simon alone."

Rick's deepest fear came to life right before his eyes, and he began to shake. "You told them?" He looked over at Spence to see his face was set in stone. *And he was pissed.* It was better this way. If he hated Rick for his past, it would be easier to separate himself from Spence and everyone else in the house.

"No, not everything. It's not my story to tell. But I did let them know someone evil is chasing you. It's your choice of how much or how little to tell the team."

"Why would they care? Other than Spence, none of them have any friendly feelings toward me."

That statement had more than one team member looking away. They couldn't deny it, and they knew it. Why did they even bother being here? Was it some team-building exercise?

When no one spoke, he continued. "There's no way I'm bringing Simon's kind of trouble here." Rick wanted that to be known straight up. "It's best if I lead him away."

"So, it is Simon. I thought so," Roman said. "How did that bastard reach you?"

"Email." What was the use in lying now? "I swear, I don't know how he found me after all these years."

"A lotta years," Roman added. "You'd think he'd lose interest."

"Yesterday, after breakfast," Spence began while moving closer. "When I found you out on the deck, I knew something was wrong. You'd just read the email."

"What did he say?" Brick asked. "And we'll need more details to track him."

Rick set down his bag. Clearly, he wasn't going anywhere. "You know the usual. Hi, how are you? Long time no see. Come back, or I'll send out Spike to retrieve you. Blah, blah, blah, from your friends."

The growl that Spence let out was impressive. "The bastard threatened to come to take you, and what? Kill anyone who gets in the way?"

"He's a cold-blooded killer. I've seen it with my own eyes," Rick stated, not wanting anyone to have any misconceptions. "Spike and all the people who work for Simon would think nothing of firing off rounds in a public setting, and have. Allowing them to come here and endangering everyone is not an option."

"How long have you been on the run?" Sheriff Elias asked.

"Fifteen years."

"Is Rick your real name?" Spence asked.

"It's my chosen name. I picked it when I started over." It was the truth, and he wished he could keep it, but he'd have to change it yet again.

"Is he some sort of psycho ex-boyfriend of yours?" Spence asked, and Rick didn't miss the dark tone in his voice. "Why the hell would you get involved with someone like that?"

"I didn't do anything willingly," Rick growled right back at him. Of course, blaming the victim wasn't new in his world, but coming from Spence, it hurt.

"I find it hard to believe someone like you doing anything you didn't want to," Spence's voice got louder. "Maybe you still have a thing for him."

"What the hell are you talking about?" For once, the rest of the team looked as confused as Rick felt. Did this have something to do with their pseudo-date?

"Wait, I'm confused," Julia said from somewhere in the kitchen. Rick hadn't even noticed her back there. "You're going back to your lover?"

"No," he said loud enough for them all to hear. "Simon isn't my old lover."

"Then who is he?" Spence asked. "Why won't he let you go?"

"Because he believes he owns me." Rick couldn't stop his voice from breaking. This was it, do-or-die time. "He was my pimp."

# CHAPTER SEVEN
*Rick*

The silence was deafening.

Rick never truly understood the impact of that statement until right now. He didn't bother taking in their expressions. He knew what disgust looked like.

Julia ran out from behind the team and took him into her arms. "Oh, honey. I'm so sorry. No one should ever have to go through that. How old were you?"

Julia's real estate boss had tried to force her to have sex with Brick to get his hands on the lake house property. She knew a touch of what he'd lived through, but Brick had been there to save her.

No one had been there to save him.

"Sixteen." The day he'd decided to give up fighting the inevitable. "Excuse me."

Rick bent and picked up his bag and turned back toward the front door. It was time to go. They had to realize that by now.

"Where the hell do you think you're going?" Roman asked.

"I'll try to reach out from wherever I land, if it's safe."

"Not a chance," Brick said. "You're staying with us until we can rectify this situation."

"Give this Simon dude what he has comin' to him," Shaw grumbled.

"Damn right," Gunner joined in.

Spence remained quiet. Obviously, Rick's fears were well founded. Who'd want a former prostitute as a boyfriend? No one was the obvious answer. He suddenly felt exhausted and wanted to crawl back into his bed upstairs, but he was a man and needed to face this head-on then get gone.

"No one has to go to bat for me. I'm no longer that sixteen-year-old boy living on the streets in Chicago. I have money saved and know a hell of a lot more about hiding than I once did. I'll disappear."

"Is that what you want?" Spence asked. "To disappear?"

Of course, he didn't. He'd grown to like his new life and the person he'd become. "There's no other choice."

"Sure there is," Spencer stated. "You stay and fight."

"And put everyone in danger? I don't think so."

"I have an idea," Fletch said. "You come with Spence, Gunner, and I on our mission. That way you're safe, and you're away from the lake house while we come up with a plan to deal with Simon."

"That might work," Brick agreed. "You'll be off the radar for a while."

"It's perfect," Roman said, his shoulders slumping. "Please. Go with the guys. You'll be away, and you'll be safe. I don't want to lose you."

Rick looked around at the people gathered and couldn't help but wonder why most of them cared, except for Roman. He loved his friend and had to consider what leaving would mean to him. If there was anyone on the planet Rick didn't want to disappoint, it was Roman.

"Okay."

***

*Spence*

He was a Grade A asshole. Spence couldn't explain what had come over him. One moment he was angry and concerned about the guy after Rick, and the next, he's accusing him of running back to his former lover. Where the hell had that come from? He could admit his anger was spawned by Rick intending to take off without a word, but that was no excuse for sounding like a jealous fucker.

After his spectacular crash and burn, Spence couldn't find his voice, and didn't say anything more to Rick. *Sorry I accused you of running back to your pimp* didn't seem to cut it. Now here he sat on a plane headed to New York in a row behind Rick and Fletcher. Gunner sat beside him. Before they'd left the lake house, Spence had worked his magic and provided Rick with a new ID to keep Simon from following him.

*Pimp.* Out of everything he'd expected Rick to say, Simon being his pimp wasn't even in the equation. He wondered how Rick went from living with his dad in Texas to being homeless at sixteen in Chicago. Spence knew that scum like Simon hunted out lost teens alone in the city and trapped them in a life they no longer had control over. After appearing to be "taken in," they were thrown out onto the street to sell themselves to pay back their pimp for an insurmountable debt they're told they owe.

It tore at him Rick had been through that kind of hell, and he'd do whatever it took to make sure Simon never got close to Rick ever again. Rick had given them the pimp's full name, Simon Relch, but not much more. At least it gave Spence a place to start.

He'd been digging into the guy only a short time when he came across a police report implicating Simon in a double homicide. Still, none of the witnesses came forward, leaving the decade-old case unsolved.

Simon's record was littered with assaults, robberies, and arson. Typical strong-arm tactics of a thug. His first arrest came at nine for stealing a car and joyriding it through a soccer field. He'd spent most of his childhood in foster care or juvie, and was set loose from both at eighteen.

He spent his adult life pretty much the same way as his youth, breaking the law and terrorizing people. A true upstanding citizen.

Hours after they'd left Texas, Spence had worked up a complete bio on the guy who'd terrorized Rick, and he was ready to hunt. They deplaned, got into their rental car, and after fighting miserable traffic, they finally arrived at their two-story, four-bedroom rental property in New Rochelle.

Putting Simon down would have to wait. They were on the clock and had a missing sixteen-year-old girl to find. To kick off the investigation, today they had interviews set up with the family members.

The air was thick between Rick and Spence as the team split up to claim a bedroom. Gunner and Fletch took the two bedrooms downstairs while Rick and Spence were upstairs. He preferred having Rick close by in case anything happened. He knew the feeling wasn't mutual, but he'd protect him with his life.

Spence dropped Rick's bag outside the room he'd chosen before heading to his own. Gunner was already checking the yard for easy access points and security measures they'd need to install.

"Thank you," Rick said, causing Spence to turn around as he made his way down the hall. "For my bag."

"You're welcome," Spence responded with a nod. "Look, I'm sorry for the way I behaved earlier. I have no excuse for being an ass." His mind went blank as he tried to come up with something more meaningful.

Rick looked up, and the pain on his face almost floored Spence. "It's okay. I understand. I'm tired. I think I'll go lie down."

Though he wasn't sure what it was that Rick understood, Spence didn't want to keep him from resting after the day he'd had. "Okay. Call me if you need anything. I'll wake you for supper."

Rick nodded, picked up his bag, and shut the bedroom door behind him.

Spence pulled himself away from Rick's door and dropped his belongings in his room before grabbing his laptop and a small bag of sensors and cameras, each about the size of a quarter. He'd place them all over the inside and outside of the house to keep an eye on things. He'd never been one for uninvited visitors, and given Rick's situation, vigilance above diligence was in order.

When Spence walked into the living room, he found Fletch already rearranging the furniture. The interviews would be conducted here in neutral territory, and then they would branch out to search Ellen's family home, her route, and her school. Whatever information they gathered would help lead them to finding her.

They removed the loveseat and set two wooden kitchen chairs in its place. The last thing they wanted was for the interviewees to get comfortable. The couch was shoved against the far wall out of the way. They'd move it back when they were done.

"Rick talking to you yet?" Fletch asked as he brought a table lamp closer to the chairs.

Spence opened the bag of sensors. "No, not really."

Fletch scanned the area before lowering his voice. "It's just us here. What the hell happened, man? I've never seen you lose your cool like that, and we've been through some crazy shit."

"I wish I knew. Something snapped, and my stupid mouth started spewing before my brain caught up."

"You accused him of sneaking away to be with his pimp."

"That was before I knew Simon had been his pimp."

"You were jealous?"

"I was angry he would take off without so much as a fuck you."

Fletch looked at him closely, which made Spence take a step back. No one needed to psychoanalyze him.

"You've fallen for him. That's why you're acting irrationally. I get it. I felt the same about Elias."

"I remember you two kissing over a packed bar in the middle of God's country Texas." Which resulted in an attempt on Fletch's life.

"Exactly," Fletch said as if that explained it all.

"You're trying to tell me I acted like a jackass because I've fallen for Rick?"

"Now you're getting it. Glad we had this talk," Fletch said as he slapped his shoulder. "I'll let you get set up in here and go help

Gunner." He walked out the patio doors without saying another word.

What the hell kind of advice was that? He wasn't any clearer when it came to Rick than before. This was why he never allowed himself to get emotional. Inevitably, everything got messed up.

Maybe it would be best to back off.

The last thing Rick needed was another idiot to worry about.

# CHAPTER EIGHT
*Rick*

Rick had stayed in his room for hours, lying on his bed staring at the ceiling, exhausted but unable to sleep. The room was clean but unimaginative: a queen bed, highboy dresser, small television on top, and an ensuite bathroom. He'd heard voices coming from downstairs and realized the air vent in his room wasn't sealed properly. There seemed to be a quarter-inch gap covered over with carpeting. Something that was never repaired. When the central air came on, the voices became garbled and almost impossible to decipher.

As he stared at the ceiling, he thought about what he'd give to undo yesterday. He wouldn't've allowed himself to go out on the boat with Spence. All this tension wouldn't be half as bad if he hadn't kissed the guy. It would be easier if he hadn't learned what it felt like to be in Spence's strong, muscled arms, knowing he'd never be in that position again. He ached for the comfort Spence had offered sharing his garden paradise on a secluded island.

Since he'd always be used goods, he knew better than to expect Spence's kindness and caring again.

Placing his forearm over his eyes, he took a deep breath and tried to redirect his thoughts. There was nothing to gain from wallowing in lament. He couldn't change his past, and Spence had every right to back away. Instead of replaying the past twenty-four hours, Rick focused on the flight to New York, and Fletcher explaining their case to him. A girl named Ellen was missing. She was only sixteen, and

Rick hoped she hadn't headed to nearby Manhattan. The city would swallow her up like Chicago had done to him all those years ago.

Roughly thirty minutes ago, the doorbell had rung and he'd overheard the introductions: the visitors were Ellen's parents, Elise and Tom. The obligatory questions were asked: *Where were you when your daughter went missing? Do you remember her being upset in the days leading up to her disappearance,* and so on?

Their answers pulled at Rick. Something felt off to him regarding their relationship with their daughter.

When they were asked about their careers, both were articulate and brimming with information. They weren't shy about self-promotion, and almost every word out of their mouths was headline ready. However, when the questions veered to more personal and private areas about their daughter, the dad zoned out and didn't sound invested in Ellen's whereabouts or safety.

They were asked: *What are Ellen's friends' names? Who does she hang out with? Does she have any outside interests away from school?*

Elise stumbled like a drunk on a two-day bender trying to answer even basic knowledge about their daughter's life, and Tom didn't seem to be able to help her.

*We work long hours or are away on business, and bills need to get paid.* The usual bullshit or she'd even go as far as to blame Ellen by saying things like: *she's a teenager, she doesn't tell me everything, her hormones were out of control, and she argues with me about everything.* Parental faults were always explained away when it was obvious that the mother knew nothing about her daughter, and Tom's lack of interest created more questions than answers.

Rick wanted to go downstairs to the living room and shake them for not treating Ellen as the most important part of their lives, but he knew better and doubted his words would affect them.

He'd leave it to the professionals even though he was dying to ask dear old dad one question, which Spence asked: "Why did you fire Ellen's nanny?"

"She was no longer needed. Ellen is a teenager able to care for herself," Tom provided.

More cold and unfeeling bullshit. Then Rick came up with an idea. He picked up his cell and typed out a message. With any luck, Spence's phone wouldn't be on mute. He heard the telltale ding of the text and thought he could be way off, but the question had to be asked.

He didn't have to wait long before Spence said, "Mr. Hammon, is Ellen your biological daughter?"

Rick heard the swift intake of breaths from the Hammons and sputtered words were followed by broken sentences.

"What the hell?" Tom huffed, but not enough to pull off shocked and offended.

"How dare you," Elise followed, as if her common decency was being questioned.

*Sorry, lady, that ship has sailed.*

Through all the blustering, Rick had yet to hear an outright denial or even an answer to the question.

"Mr. Hammon, answer the question," Gunner directed in a stern voice. In truth, he was a softy to those who knew him, but the big guy could be crazy scary when he needed to be.

"You may want to bear in mind we will dig until we have answers. Either work with us, or you never know what might be splashed across the internet," Spence stated in his "I don't take shit" tone. Rick couldn't help but smile.

For a brief moment, he allowed himself to bask in the glow that Spence had trusted him enough to ask the question. Rick had been front row center for his own "not blood related" saga after his father died, and he learned his extended family deemed him unacceptable to be cared for.

"Ellen doesn't know," Elise said in a hushed voice.

"Who's the father?" Fletch asked.

Silence.

"Do you know who the father is?" Spence asked.

"It could be one of three men," Elise admitted.

"We'll need their names," Gunner stated. "The local PD did a DNA workup on Ellen. We'll need that in order to figure out who the father is."

"Wait just a minute. You were called in to find Ellen." Tom blustered. "Not start a media frenzy over indiscretions decades old."

"Yeah. We don't want to forget about your love child either, Tom."

"I don't know what you're talking about."

*Oh shit. Things are about to get crazy.* Rick pressed his ear closer to the vent, not wanting to miss a word, when the central air-conditioning decided it was time to cool everyone down and effectively ended Rick's participation in the proceedings.

He went back and lay on the bed, and it wasn't long before his eyes were closing. Of course, now he wanted to stay awake to hear more, but his body had other ideas.

\*\*\*

*Spence*

Spence headed for the stairs as soon as the door closed behind the Hammons. He had to talk with Rick, and it couldn't wait.

"Hey, good catch on the paternity issue," Fletch said.

"It wasn't me. Rick must've overheard the questioning and sent me a text to ask."

"Rick?" Gunner asked.

"Yep. The guy saw straight through Tom. I knew something was up with the father, but Rick put the fine point on it." Spence wanted to know how and why he easily picked up on that clue.

"So, both parents have love children, but not together?"

"Looks like."

"Damn. Why did they stay married?"

"Ratings. Their fledgling morning show was moving up the charts. One, let alone two, scandals would've spelled the end for both of them."

"Who do we have coming next?"

"Jacob, in about forty minutes."

"Great," Spence grumbled. The last thing he needed was a reunion with a former lover. "I'll be back."

Spence took the stairs two at a time and stopped outside Rick's closed door. He knocked once and heard nothing, knocked again, and still silence. Quietly he turned the knob and opened the door wide enough to allow him to slide through. The room wasn't dark as the drapes were wide open. He could see Rick lying on his side, his blond hair tousled, and his blue-framed glasses were sitting on the side table alongside a bottle of water.

He didn't have the heart to wake him and turned to step out the door.

"How'd it go?" Rick asked groggily.

Spence stopped and looked back to find Rick pushing at the pillows to sit up, and then reaching for his glasses. No one had the right to look that gorgeous waking up. When he bothered to look up while brushing his teeth in the morning, Spence looked like he'd been hit by a truck. Hair standing on end, lines from the pillow engraved on his face, and dried evidence of drool all over his chin.

"Quite an enlightening interview. I have a clearer image of Ellen's home life now."

"Yeah. It doesn't sound like the white picket fence and rose garden existence they portray in media. I feel sorry for the kid."

"The more I learn, the more I suspect the girl took off, but to where?" Spence leaned against the highboy. "Thanks for your insightful question."

"You're welcome."

"Maybe we should have you downstairs with us during the remaining interviews," he joked. "How'd you know?"

"It wasn't hard for me to pick up on the disconnect. I've heard it before."

"Before?"

Rick looked at him as if unsure whether to carry on, and Spence couldn't blame him considering his boneheaded reaction earlier.

"You don't have to tell me. I believe you know how to sense these things, and that's good enough." He shook his head. "Gotta say, it certainly shook things up."

Rick laughed. "I thought the guy was going to blow. So much for their squeaky-clean personas."

"Yeah, I get the feeling that's all over now."

Spence waited patiently while Rick seemed to be gathering his thoughts. Finally, he said, "I knew he wasn't Ellen's real father because my stepmother, Cheryl, behaved the same way: detached, unemotional, and bored. Before the wedding, she seemed like a nice enough lady, but, apparently, she wasn't. In the time between her marrying my dad and him dying, the house and all his assets became hers. I had my clothes, my personal savings, which wasn't much, and she couldn't wait to throw me out of the house. None of my extended family was interested in taking me in. Within a week of my father's death, I was two months shy of sixteen and homeless. She moved on as if I never existed and married some other guy eight months after my dad died."

"I'm so sorry." Spence's gut reaction was to go out and find this woman and fuck with her life twice as hard as she'd done to Rick. "How'd your father die?"

"Car accident. I was away at school when it happened."

"Shit, man, and she threw you out onto the streets? Some humans don't deserve the lives they've been given." Spence's heart ached for the young Rick who'd been abandoned, scared, and alone.

Rick shrugged. "I imagine you've seen your fair share of shitty people in your line of work."

"I've seen the worst in humanity and the best, but the lengths people go to get what they want never ceases to amaze me. I've seen bombs hidden inside the dead bodies of women and children so the rescuers would be killed when they came in to help. I've seen decent men become shells of their former selves due to war's violent and inhumane realities."

"How about you? Do you suffer from those kinds of memories?"

"I have moments when I can't fight them off."

"The island. That's where you go when the memories become too much."

Spence nodded. "It's my way of escaping in a place that reminds me beauty and serenity exist."

"An escape."

They were back to enjoying the ease they'd shared on the island, but it was cut short by the front doorbell.

Jacob had arrived.

# CHAPTER NINE
*Spence*

By the time Spence made it downstairs, Jacob was sitting in one of the living room chairs. It'd been over a decade since Spence had seen his former lover, and it was still too soon. His look had changed from a clean-shaven Navy corpsman to an unshaven, dreadlocked, Southern California beach bum.

His pants were torn in places, and not the stylish type of rips. His heavy metal band t-shirt was faded, and he was wearing flip-flops that looked molded to his feet. Though there wasn't a beach in sight, Jacob was ready to catch the next wave. All he needed was a surfboard. According to his employment record, he worked as a chef, but Spence wasn't sure he'd eat anything coming out of this guy's kitchen.

"Hey, handsome, wondered where you were hiding," Jacob said as soon as he caught sight of Spence. "You left me here with these gorillas."

Instead of acknowledging a word the guy had said, Spence stated, "You're here to answer questions regarding your niece's disappearance. The sooner you answer, the quicker you can be on your way."

Jacob leaned back in the chair and adjusted his dick. "I know what you want. Three-one-zero—"

"What the hell is that?" Fletch asked before Jacob could finish.

"It's my cell phone number," Jacob said as he leered at Spence.

"We already have your number, it's in the police file," Gunner stated. "We need to know your relationship with your niece and if you have any idea where she might be."

Spence was happy for the backup because he doubted he'd be able to keep his cool around the jerk. A sixteen-year-old girl was missing, and her uncle wanted to hook up instead of help out.

"When was the last time you saw or spoke to Ellen?" Spence asked.

"Christmas Day."

"So roughly six months ago."

"Yeah. I called her to wish her a Merry Christmas like I do every year," Jacob said. "My turn. Whatcha doing later tonight, Spence?"

"None of your business. Get your head on straight. Did Ellen seem any different when you spoke with her? Was she stressed or happy?"

"I used to be your business, lover boy."

*For fuck's sake.* Spence stood and was about to excuse himself since it was obvious the guy wouldn't stop messing with him when he heard footsteps on the staircase behind him.

Moments later, Rick came storming into the room. "You skanky slut. A young girl is missing, and all your lice-infested head can think about is sex. This isn't a game, you pissant. A life is on the line. Stop fucking around, or I'll cut those dreads off one at a time."

To stress the point, he produced a pair of scissors, and before anyone could stop him, Rick snipped off one particularly large dreadlock that made a thud when it hit the floor.

"What the hell? You cut my hair."

"I'll cut more if you keep this shit up," Rick growled.

Perfect. Spence wasn't able hide his smirk. This was the Rick he knew. "Did Ellen seem odd or off when you called her last Christmas?"

Jacob looked between him and Rick. "You can't do this."

*Snip. Thud.*

"She was sad, okay?" Jacob turned to Rick. "Knock it off, man. Don't cut anymore." Then he focused on Spence. "Ellen was depressed," he said in a rush while trying to cover the rest of his hair with his hands.

"Did she tell you why she was sad?" Gunner asked.

"With her parents. It could've been any number of things."

"What do you mean by that?" Rick asked as he raised the scissors. "Try to be specific."

"Have you met them? Christ, they were away doing some damn holiday special in Maui. No, that was the year before. St. Lucia last year. Either way, Ellen was alone again. She talked about the lady who cooks for them inviting her to have Christmas with her family."

"Did she go?"

"I don't know. I invited her to come out to California, but we both knew that wasn't possible."

"Why?" Spence asked.

"Her parents didn't want her to hang around her gay uncle from a previous marriage. Since Elise and I have different mothers, I'm not considered part of the family. I'm not good enough."

"What a bitch," Rick said as he lowered the scissors.

"You don't know the half of it. Those two never should've had a child. They're horrible at it. And then they fire her nanny, the only constant in the kid's life. Fucked-up people."

"You know why they fired the nanny?" Gunner asked.

"No. Neither did Ellen when I asked. She told me Rosaline left one day and never came back."

"What do you think happened to Ellen?" Spence asked.

"The kid took off. She couldn't take it anymore. I think my half-sister's staff would be the best people to ask. They were there every day, and believe me, they were mostly ignored. They're like flies on the wall, soaking in information and every salacious detail. I suspect a tell-all is in the works."

Spence agreed that fit the parents' MO. Employees weren't worth their notice. He'd have to dig into the possible tell-all to see if there were any offers out there or contracts signed.

After a couple more questions, they had a few lines to tug, which was more than what Spence had thought would come from this meeting.

"Look, Spence. I'm sorry for what my father tried to do to you."

Spence hadn't seen that coming. "It was long ago."

"Yeah, but I never apologized to you personally."

"What did your dad do?" Rick set the scissors down on the table.

"After my commander father found out I'd slept with Spence, he went crazy trying to destroy him and his military career. It didn't matter how many other people I slept with. I couldn't get him to un-fixate from Spence. The old man blamed him for everything I did after that no matter what I said or did."

Spence hadn't known Jacob's promiscuity after they'd broken up was an attempt to distract Commander Rask from his mission to see Spence dishonorably discharged or jailed. He'd never have guessed. Then again, he'd been quantum pissed at the time.

Before he could respond, there was a loud knock on the front door.

"Rask isn't due for another hour," Gunner said as he flicked through various cameras on the monitor. "Yep, it's him."

"An hour early," Rick said.

"Totally his style. Likes to throw everyone off," Spence grumbled. "I should've seen it coming."

"My father's here?" Jacob asked, his voice cracked at a higher pitch. "I can't see him. I moved to the other side of the country so I'd never run into him again."

The team glanced at one another, then Spence said, "Okay, this is what we're going to do." Spence turned. "Rick, you take Jacob into the laundry room. There's a door leading into the backyard from there. When I give you the signal, Jacob, make a run for your car. We'll keep Rask in the living room."

Jacob stood from the chair, and Rick took his hand. "It'll be okay. Let's go. What's the signal?"

"I'll go into the kitchen and ask if Rask wants coffee."

"Got it."

A second round of pounding on the front door had them moving. When Spence heard the laundry room door close, he headed for the front door.

"You want me to get that, man?" Fletch lifted his chin.

"Nah. I got this. The days of Rask holding any power over me are long over."

With a final look around the room, Spence plastered a smile on his face and opened the door.

***

*Rick*

Jacob huddled close to the side door while Rick stood against the laundry room door, listening for the sign. He could feel the man's fear radiating in the small room.

"It'll be okay," Rick whispered. "The team won't let your father near you."

"Thanks," Jacob replied. "How long you and Spence been together?'

Rick shook his head. "We're not a couple."

"Really? Have you seen the way he looks at you?"

"I'm just another case, that's all."

"I wouldn't be too sure of that," Jacob whispered back. "He's a good guy, you know."

"I do know." It was one of the only things he knew for certain.

"And one hell of a catch."

"Seriously?" Rick groaned.

Jacob's expression changed, and for the first time, Rick felt like he was meeting the real man. "Spence's a stand-up guy and deserved a whole lot better than he got. Give him a chance."

Rick was at a loss for words, but hearing Spence's voice in the kitchen put him on alert.

"You want coffee, Rask?"

"Good luck finding Ellen. I really hope she's okay," Jacob said before he opened the back door and slipped out.

Rick stood there for several minutes trying to organize his thoughts before stepping into the house. He agreed with Jacob on one point: Spence deserved better, which didn't include Rick, no matter how he looked at him.

He gathered his shields around him and stepped into the kitchen to find Spence pouring a single cup of coffee. The other three had to be in the living room around the corner.

"Everything okay?" Spence asked as he joined him at the counter.

"All good. He's long gone." Rick got a whiff of the coffee. "That doesn't smell right, you know."

"I do." Spence smiled wide. "Thanks for helping hide him and keeping Jacob on track throughout his interview."

"It's amazing what wielding a pair of scissors can do. I was ready to shave him bald if I had to. There's a young girl's life at stake."

Spence moved closer, and for a brief moment Rick thought Spence was going to pull him in for a hug, but he stopped.

"Agreed," Spence said before stepping back. "I would like you to join us for Rask's interview. You seem to have your finger on the pulse of this case, having lived through something similar."

"You guys know what you're doing, but I'd still like to be there." Rick needed to help find Ellen before her life was destroyed as his had been.

"Good. That's what I was hoping you'd say."

Spence picked up the mug and led the way into the living room. The hulking stranger sitting on one of the chairs in the middle of the room had to be Commander Rask. He looked less than impressed and didn't mind letting everyone know it. His lips were a slash across his wrinkled face, while his piercing dark eyes scanned the room. His firmly crossed arms communicated the defensive wall Rick was sure the commander was going for.

Once he had his coffee, Rask took a sip and turned up his nose at the brew. "Where'd you get this shit? It tastes like bathwater." He jabbed his thick finger at Rick. "And who the hell are you?"

"It's a special brew called whatever the rental house has in the cupboard. Don't act like you haven't had worse. And, while it's none of your business, Rick is part of L.H. Investigations," Spence replied in a firm tone. Clearly, Rask respected power, and in this situation, Spence held all of it. Rask had no rank over Spence, and no matter how much crap he spewed, it wouldn't change the dynamic.

Which bothered the hell out of Rask, especially when he didn't get the rise out of Spence he'd undoubtedly hoped for. His gray hair was cut high and tight, while dog tags peeked out from under his button-up shirt. There was a bulge on the inside of his left ankle—a clutch piece. As if he'd need a firearm here. The asshole probably wore it everywhere.

"Now that the pleasantries are out of the way, let's get down to it. Where do you think Ellen is?" Spence asked.

Rask cleared his throat and stated, "With Jacob, of course."

"Of course," Rick blurted out in shock. So much for staying on the sidelines. "Where did you get that idea?"

Fletcher quickly added, "The police have cleared your son. His alibi checks out, and he allowed officers to search his apartment. Ellen wasn't there, and there were no signs she ever had been."

"He's the only deviant in the family with access to Ellen. He must've convinced her to go to California and live with the hippies, tree huggers, and whackos."

"Deviant? You mean gay?" Spence asked in a voice so calm he could have been meditating.

"Yeah. You'd know a lot about that," Rask growled. "Your dress swings that way."

"Don't you want to find your granddaughter?" Rick asked, totally baffled by the man in front of him.

"Of course I do," Rask said with a sneer of disgust.

"Then why are you allowing your bigotry to cloud your common sense?"

"When was the last time you spoke to Ellen?" Spence asked before Rask could respond to Rick's question.

"A couple of days before she disappeared. And let's get one thing straight, I didn't want your group here. I still don't. If it weren't for the police chief's friendship with your Lieutenant Commander Brick, I'd never have to set eyes on you fuckups again."

"Noted. How did she seem to you?" Gunner questioned, keeping things on track. "What did you talk about?"

"Seem? Like she always does, busy with school and friends. Ellen called me when she couldn't reach her parents."

"Why couldn't she reach her parents?" Fletch asked while taking notes on the iPad in front of him.

"They were out of town for a charity event and had their phones in flight mode."

"Why was she trying to reach them?" Spence asked.

"I don't know."

"You didn't ask her? What if she needed help?" Rick was unable to keep the alarm out of his voice.

"She was fine," Rask said as if the questions were completely unnecessary. "Teenage girl problems."

"Do you know any of her friends?" Spence carried on with the questioning.

"No."

"How often did you see Ellen?"

"A couple of times a year."

"Holidays?"

"Yes."

"How was your granddaughter's home life?" That's where their back-and-forth ended.

Rask's expression darkened, if that were even possible. "Idyllic. She has everything she ever wanted and goes to the best schools. She's probably doing this for attention. Ellen's always been needy."

"I'm sure she had access to the best of things," Spence agreed, outwardly calm, but Rick knew he had to be boiling inside. The asshole was trying to blame the missing girl for her own disappearance. "However, I'm more concerned with her emotional health."

"Emotional health? What kinda bullshit are you talking about? This is how you intend to find my granddaughter? Maybe we should all hold hands, you fluffy fag."

"It has to be small dick syndrome," Rick stated. It was time to put this fucker in his place.

"What the fuck?" Rask thundered as he stood.

Spence moved lightning fast to stand in front of Rick. "Not a chance, old man."

Rick carried on with his commentary. "Well, it makes sense. He's overcompensating for something, and you have to wonder after three wives where the problem is. It's either below the waist or he's hiding something."

"Which is it, Rask?" Gunner asked, his right hand resting on the sidearm attached to his belt. Fletch stood at the ready, waiting for Rask to make a move to his concealed gun.

Rask looked around at the four of them as if they were insane. Slowly, he sat back in the chair and recrossed his arms when no one budged.

"I'm not hiding anything."

"Then why are you lying about Ellen and her family?" Spence asked as he returned to his chair as well.

The muscles on the sides of Rask's jaw began to tic as the seconds dragged on, and Rick was sure the guy was trying to decide whether to leave. He'd appear weak if he ran away, and Rick knew that would never do, not with the history between him and the team.

"Maybe they aren't the best parents in the world. That's not a crime," the former commander admitted. "They have to work. It's not as if they could stay at home all the time," Rask defended.

"From my research, over the last fifty-two weeks, Tom and Elise spent over thirty-six of those away from their daughter," Spence was quick to point out. "That's extreme by anyone's standards."

"They have an image to keep up," Rask defended.

"Seriously? They wanted to portray the perfect image of the American family. Money, careers, celebrity, a mansion on the hill, staff, and the proper, educated daughter at home. When in truth, their lives were built on a lie. Hell, they both have a child, but not with each other," Fletcher said.

"That sounds more American than the shit they're shoveling," Gunner confirmed.

"By your lack of surprise," Spence announced, "you knew Tom isn't Ellen's father."

"I do and I did."

"When did you find out?"

"Elise told me when she was pregnant."

"This was after Tom's affair, correct?"

"Yes."

"Was it a tit-for-tat kinda thing?"

"Yes."

"And Tom went with it?"

"They were on the short list of couples up for the television station's new morning show."

"So, adding she was pregnant and could relate to a larger demographic, namely moms, didn't hurt their chances of winning the job."

"No, it didn't."

"What do you know about Tom's love child?"

"Dylan."

"You know him?"

"I've kept an eye on the situation."

"The situation? You mean his birth?"

"Yeah. The mother was paid handsomely for her silence, and I wanted to ensure it stayed that way."

"How old would Dylan be now? Eighteen?"

"Nineteen."

"We'll need everything you've got on Dylan," Gunner interjected.

Rask nodded. "Are we done?"

"I have a few more questions. If we take Jacob off the table, where do you think Ellen may have gone?"

"She had a close relationship with her grandmother, June."

"Your second wife?"

"Yes, but June passed a few months ago. If she were alive, I'd say to start there, but as it stands, I don't know."

"Since retiring, what have you been doing to fill your days?"

"I keep busy around the house." His arms crossed even tighter, the lying sack of shit.

"You're telling me you walked away from a lifetime spent in the Navy to sit on your lawnmower? I don't buy it."

"I don't give a shit what you believe."

"If you were taking on side jobs or consulting positions, is there any chance someone targeted your granddaughter?"

"I have no idea what you're talking about. You done?"

"Disappointing, but not surprising. I thought you'd 'fess up to save your granddaughter, but it doesn't matter. I'm exceptionally good at what I do. We'll be in touch," Spence said as Rask stood. "Gunner will show you out."

Rask turned to face the front door but stopped. "If your team's half as good as they say you guys are, you'll find Ellen before irreparable damage is done. I'm counting on that."

Rick watched his retreating figure, still at a loss for how truly messed up the old man's family was. He was beginning to see things from Ellen's point of view and understood why she might've left.

When Rick heard the door close, the tension in the room subsided and everyone looked less tense.

"You okay?" Spence asked as he drew nearer.

"Yeah. I just feel so badly for that poor girl."

"I think we can all agree on that." Fletch sighed. "I'm ordering takeout for dinner. How's Chinese food?"

"Sure," Rick agreed without pointing out the higher sodium, sugar, and trans fats in restaurant food. He wondered if he should tell Fletch to make sure they didn't put MSG in the food.

"Yeah," Spence replied.

"I'm good with that. Don't forget the beer," Gunner said as he pulled out his cell and headed for the hallway. "I need to speak with Ben."

Rick understood why Gunner felt such a strong need to touch base with his nephew. After the stellar parenting they'd been confronted with this afternoon, the need to make certain Ben knew he was loved had to be pressing hard on Gunner.

"He's a good man," Rick said as Gunner disappeared.

"You have no idea." Spence nodded. "When there's time, I'll tell you a few stories."

"Hey, buddy, how's my favorite nephew?" Rick heard a few words before Gunner shut his bedroom door.

Rick couldn't help but compare the loving parents routine the Hammons tried to pull off with the true love and concern Gunner was showing for his dead sister's son.

Particularly upsetting was that certain groups believed the Hammons' parenting was preferable to a gay man caring for a child simply because they were hetero.

How had the world become so cold?

# CHAPTER TEN

*Spence*

The kitchen smelled delicious as plates were filled and refilled with Kung Pao chicken, sweet and sour pork, dumplings, chow mein, vegetable fried rice, and so much more. His team could eat. Spence was on his second plate and was finally beginning to feel full. When the food arrived, they acted as if they were starving for days and dug in, ditching any talk until after they'd had their fill.

It'd been a long day, and it was hard to believe Rick had attempted to leave only that morning without telling anyone. Now they were in New York, three interviews down and more to come while searching for a girl and protecting Rick from Simon. Everyone was exhausted, but they still needed to run through what they had found out so far.

He looked around to confirm his team members had slowed their eating and were ready to recap. "Okay, let's go over what we've learned." The men began listing things off.

"Tom is not Ellen's father. We have a list of three possible sperm donors."

"Dylan is Tom Hammon's nineteen-year-old love child."

"The Hammons sucked at being parents and used the pregnancy to win the spot on the morning show. We should check in on the other couples who were up for the job. Revenge isn't off the table."

"Rask hasn't changed a bit," Fletcher added. "Still a complete asshole."

"His second wife died recently. We need to find out how that went down."

"We're missing a former nanny, Rosaline."

"Questioning the house staff is the logical next step."

"Agreed. We'll go over to the house tomorrow and look around, then head to the school."

"Any information on the driver's felony conviction?" Gunner asked.

"Grand theft auto. Joseph Allen did almost two years but was released on good behavior, and he's been clean since," Spence answered.

"Rask is likely taking on military consulting jobs, but we don't know with whom," Fletch added.

"As far as first days go, it's not a bad start, but time is of the essence," Gunner stated before taking in another mouthful of food.

"Let's not forget Rask has a small dick," Rick said with a laugh, and the others joined in.

"I can't believe you said that to him." Fletch chuckled. "It took a hell of a lot of self-control not to laugh in front of the guy."

"It was time to shake him up a little. His smug attitude bothered me."

Fletch looked over at Rick. "How did you suspect Tom wasn't Ellen's biological father?"

Rick had explained to Spence, but there'd been no time to fill the team members in before Jacob showed up. "It's okay if you don't want to talk about it."

"Thank you," Rick said. "Now that my truth is out there, I don't mind sharing my insights." After having them learn about Simon and what he was to Rick, there wasn't much worse he could share. "My dad remarried when I was younger, but he died shortly after they got married, leaving me as her responsibility. I felt and heard the same cold, detached emotions today with Tom as I did with my stepmother when she was deciding my fate."

"I'm taking it didn't go well," Fletcher said.

"No, she wasn't what you'd call 'maternal,' and a week later I was out on my ass in the middle of Chicago. I wasn't quite sixteen yet."

"That's how Simon found you," Gunner stated.

"Yeah. It doesn't take long for fresh meat to be picked up. I lasted almost three months working odd jobs to buy food and sleeping at the homeless shelters across town. Which weren't any safer than being out on the sidewalks, but there was a lesser chance of being attacked by roaming dogs or rats, and other creatures that come out at night."

"Fuck, what a bitch. She dumped you like you were nothing," Gunner growled.

Rick nodded, and Spence could feel the pain of rejection as if it were his own.

"There was something wrong with her, not you," Spence said, hoping he could see that.

"I wish we could run across her path now," Gunner added. "I'd love to have a few words with her."

"Thanks, but I've learned there's no use in looking back. If anything, I'm hoping what I've been through helps us find Ellen."

"Thanks, and I swear we'll deal with Simon," Spence stated. "No one will ever get the chance to hurt you again."

"Damn right," the others joined in.

"First, we need to find Ellen before we can worry about me. She's in danger out there alone."

"We'll find her, and in the meantime, I think it would be best if Rick continues helping on the case," Spence said. "Also, I've confirmed no one of Ellen's description has turned up at the local shelters and soup kitchens."

"She's laying low. She has help or has been kidnapped, even if the local PD believes it's a long shot."

"Could Ellen's biological father have reached out to her?" Rick asked.

"Anything's possible. But Elise wasn't sure which of the three men it was who fathered her child," Gunner responded.

"So she says. Her word isn't worth the air she breathes," Fletch stated, and Spence had to agree.

"And here I thought my life was screwed up," Rick said with a harsh laugh. "This family has more skeletons in their closets than a dozen medical schools."

"You don't think they got rid of her?" Fletch asked. "Do you?"

"God, I hope not. But nothing can be ruled out until we find her," Spence said reluctantly. He didn't want that to be a possibility, but he'd seen and experienced worse and knew humans were capable of incredible cruelty.

"Maybe she found out the truth and threatened to go public," Fletch offered.

"It's possible, and that might be motive enough for those two parents of the year to do something drastic."

"I'm curious to hear what the staff has to say about all this," Rick said. "I remember going unseen on the streets, and it always amazed me what people would do and say right in front of me."

"I'll be digging into offers for a tell-all later tonight. Best to go in with an ace up our sleeves."

"Agreed."

With a plan in the works, the men finished their meals and moved on to securing the house for the night while Spence pulled out old faithful, his state-of-the-art laptop hidden in the shell of an older generation laptop that gave none of its secrets away. Only he knew how to bring its true power to life. He adjusted his desktop satellite dish and brought the beast to life.

"Is there anything I can do to help?" Rick asked as Spence set his computer on the kitchen counter. "That's quite the setup you got there."

"My pride and joy." He smirked. "And yes," he said while handing Ellen's file to Rick. "I need you to get inside this girl's head, and you're the perfect person for the job."

"I'll try, but I can't guarantee anything."

"I'm not looking for guarantees, but more of the same you pulled off today would be helpful."

"I can do that," Rick said with a nod.

It didn't surprise Spence that Rick wanted to help. He'd been doing that around the lake house for over a year. Now maybe a few others living there could see the truth of who he really was beneath all that starched armor he wore. Spence respected everything Rick had done, and he had a feeling the team did too.

"Look, I know I said this already, but I want you to know, I'm *really* sorry for being such an absolute asshole earlier today."

"It's okay," Rick said without looking at him.

"If I have an excuse for my behavior, it's my jealousy and pain over what I heard. It surprised me, and my mouth got away from me."

Rick looked up from the file. "Jealous?" Those perfectly tended eyebrows scrunched together, and for the first time, Spence wondered if Rick's highly polished appearance was another defense mechanism.

"Yeah, I couldn't understand why you would get up and leave, so I jumped to conclusions about what this guy meant to you."

"You were jealous of Simon?"

"Yeah, but before I knew the full story. I knew you were sneaking off after our kiss. So my brain wasn't exactly firing on all cylinders."

"It's okay. It wasn't as if I was forthcoming about my life and why I was leaving. Then I tried to sneak out before anyone got up. Don't worry. I don't blame you. The whole thing had to be a bit shocking," Rick said while raising his right hand for a shake. "Friends."

Spence took Rick's hand and pulled him closer, meeting him halfway across the table. "There's more than friendship between you and me, but if that's where you need to start, I'm good with waiting."

Rick looked surprised, but the sound of an alarm going off stopped whatever more was about to be said. Spence stood, grabbed Rick, and led him to the stairs.

"Go up to your room and lock the door while we check this out."

Spence didn't wait for a reply and took off at a run for the monitors, grabbing his Glock from the kitchen. Fletch came running in the back door, his weapon also drawn.

"Where's it coming from?"

Spence scanned the monitors until he caught sight of two figures facing off on the west side of the house. One looked to be Gunner. "There they are. Stay and protect Rick," Spence ordered before running out of the patio door and into the night.

He rounded the corner of the house to find Gunner and another man involved in a fistfight. Spence holstered his weapon and dove at the stranger, taking him to the ground with a thud. Before the guy could move, he flipped him onto his stomach and dug his knee into his back while restraining him with a zip tie around his wrists.

Gunner pulled out his flashlight and shined it at the guy's face. "What the fuck are you doing here?"

Spence was caught off guard because it sounded as though Gunner knew the guy. "Who the hell is this idiot?"

"Ben's uncle, on his father's side," Gunner growled.

*What?*

"Let me go," the guy hissed.

"No." Spence wasn't moving until he had some answers. "Why are you here?"

"I have something to deliver to Gunner."

"In the middle of the night and without using the front door. How did you know where to look?"

"It's not that hard to hire a PI to follow him around."

"Why are you following me?"

"To deliver important papers from Mom and Dad."

"Let him go, Spence," Gunner grunted.

Spence released the guy, stood him up, took out his pocketknife, and snapped off the zip tie before standing between the asshole and Gunner. "Is this fuck for real?"

"Unfortunately. What do you want, Dave?"

The guy dusted off his clothing, but those grass stains were never coming out of those knees, giving Spence a bit of satisfaction. Dave reached into his jacket, putting him and Gunner on alert even though he knew the guy wasn't carrying. For them, it was an automatic response.

"This is for you," Dave said as he held out a beige-colored envelope to Gunner.

Gunner didn't move to take it. "You assholes aren't getting him."

"Ben is better off with his grandparents," Dave argued.

"And my sister's life insurance has nothing to do with it?" Gunner's hands were balled into fists, and Spence knew he was doing everything to stay rooted to the spot.

"Wait, you're here to serve him with court papers for custody of Ben?" Spence was quickly getting up to speed.

Dave threw the envelope at Gunner's feet. "You've been served."

Spence took a single step forward, effectively wiping that grin off Dave's hawk-like face. "Go before I call the cops, asshole."

"See you in court," Dave jeered.

The guy took off running to the street, and moments later, the sound of an engine started before he pulled away.

Spence turned to find Gunner staring at the envelope as if it were preparing to attack and bent down to retrieve it for his friend.

"I'm sorry about this, man, but don't think for a minute that they're going to get custody of Ben. They picked a battle with the wrong people."

Gunner took the envelope but didn't bother to open it. "What if they're right? Ben might be better off with a family."

"You're the family that little boy needs." Spence had seen the way Ben looked at his Uncle Gunner. Total love and trust. There was no way he'd allow anyone to come between them and break that bond.

His friend sucked in a deep breath and let it out slowly. "I hope you're right."

***

*Rick*

More fucked-up family issues. Rick felt horrible for Gunner and Ben, having to face off with the paternal grandparents for custody. The two were finally settling and were getting back on their feet after Ben's mother's death, and now this happened.

Ben's mom, Mandy, had named Gunner, her brother, as the boy's legal guardian. Rick wondered what the grandparents had up their sleeves, and no one had ever mentioned Ben's father. Was he dead as well?

After settling, Rick chose to stay in his room while reading through Ellen's file. He wasn't hiding, but Spence's admission had him slightly freaked out. Jealous over someone from his past—of course before knowing who and what Simon was—and then announcing his intentions hadn't changed was...astounding.

It was much easier when he thought Spence was backing away from him. At least then he could keep his feelings under check with the knowledge that they didn't have a chance after his "big reveal."

Flattered though he may be, he knew a former street kid and prostitute was not what Spence needed, no matter what he said. Rick had to keep that front and center in his mind. After escaping Simon, he'd lived his life as best he could, and helped people when he was able. And although he knew he wasn't the beaten and bruised boy standing in the darkest alleys waiting on his next john to show up, sometimes he went there and it took time to come back from it.

Hell, if Simon had his way, Rick would be dead soon enough, and none of his emotional turmoil would matter.

Yet another heartache, but reality sucked. He knew that better than most.

# CHAPTER ELEVEN
*Rick*

Last night, he'd stayed up late reading Ellen's file and Googled her semi-famous parents. A few things stood out, and he hoped the team could explain them.

He headed downstairs at the smell of coffee. He'd been up and showered for a while, but was reviewing his notes.

"'Morning, Rick," Spence said from the kitchen while Gunner and Fletch talked on their phones. "How'd you sleep?"

"Good enough. You?"

"Not too much, but I managed to drum up some new information I think you'll find interesting."

"Really? Do we wait for the guys to finish their calls?"

"They already know. Besides, Gunner's talking to Brick about the in-law situation."

"Oh, good. We need to get him the best family lawyer out there. Roman may be able to get a referral through the company's corporate lawyers."

"I hope so. What do you want in your coffee?"

Remembering yesterday's brew, Rick was quick to ask, "Is this the same stuff you served Rask?"

"Hell no." Spence chuckled. "I'd never serve that to you."

"Okay. Cream and sugar, please."

Rick went over to the table and sat down with Ellen's file in front of him. He could hear Gunner's tone change when Ben came on the line. There was no doubt Gunner loved his nephew completely and would do anything to make the boy happy.

"Here you go," Spence said as he sat down and handed Rick a mug.

He took a sip of the coffee without reservation, having no doubt that Spence had told him the truth. It was heavenly, and he quickly took a second sip.

"Did anything in the file catch your attention?" Spence asked.

"Yep, and I have a few questions," Rick replied as he opened the photo gallery on his phone. "I was researching the parents and noticed someone who keeps appearing in the background of Elise and Tom's photos."

Spence moved his chair closer as Rick flicked through seven photos taken over the last twelve months. In the background was a woman wearing glasses and a headset.

"That's their manager, Susan Stapleton."

"Okay, that makes sense. Now, look at these last few taken less than a month ago." He moved to the next pictures and waited to see if Spence noticed the same thing he had.

"That's a serious amount of hatred."

"Exactly what I thought. The lady looks happy until these last snaps where she looks ready to rip Elise's and Tom's heads off."

"We have a meeting with her today. Why don't we ask her?"

"I think you should," Rick agreed. "Also, there were pictures of Ellen's room as it was left when she disappeared." He opened the file and took out the set of six pictures. "By all accounts, it looks like a typical teenage girl's room. She has a pile of colorful pillows on her canopy bed, shag throw rugs, a closet full of bright, fun clothing, the usual schoolbooks, stuffed animals, and the rest."

"Agreed, the room looks like a rainbow exploded inside it."

He couldn't help but smile at Spence's description. "Right. Then tell me what this is?" Rick asked as he pointed out a small black mark on the wall near the floor next to the dresser. "Everything else is immaculate. What's this mark doing there?"

Spence thought about it for a bit as he flipped through the pictures. Rick waited patiently to learn if he was overreacting or if it was something out of place. It could be a simple scuff mark, and it didn't take long before he doubted himself. "It's probably nothing."

"No, I don't believe it is. You're right. It stands out compared to the rest of the room. There's always a chance she was taken from her room, and it was cleaned up afterward, but they missed this spot."

"I didn't even think of that," Rick admitted. "Could the staff have something to do with this?"

"I don't know, but we're going to find out."

"What did you learn from your research?"

"I did some digging through some old Navy records and found a reference to a project that had its funding cut fourteen years ago named The Noah Project."

"What did that involve?"

"That's the thing. I couldn't find it mentioned any place else. It's been scrubbed clean from the official records, and I'm guessing I only found this one mention because someone involved didn't want it to disappear completely. I've put out a few feelers."

"Noah? Other than the biblical reference, I have no idea what that means."

"It could be a person or an anacronym or something scrubbed from the books. I also dug into the driver's background and discovered he and a bunch of teenagers were riding around in a stolen car when the police caught up with them, and they were all charged, even though our guy was in the backseat and claimed he didn't know the vehicle was stolen."

"Do you believe him?"

"No. I believe he knew it was stolen even if he wasn't the one who stole it. The car belonged to a judge, and I'm sure that didn't earn them any favor."

"I also found the PI who'd been hired to follow Gunner," Spence said in a much lower voice.

Rick looked toward the living room, finding both men still on their phones, and moved closer to Spence. "What did you do?" The smell of his cologne was intoxicating, or was it Spence's scent? It didn't matter how badly Rick wanted to kiss the handsome man in front of him again. He forced himself to hold firm to his control.

Spence's smile said it all. "The ambulance chaser's license has been revoked."

"You guys ready to head over to the Hammons' home?" Gunner asked as he came up behind them, making Rick jump. "Sorry, man."

"How can someone as big as you make no noise?" Rick asked. The sniper was like a ghost.

"Years and years of training." He laughed.

"Let's get this show on the road," Fletch said as he joined them.

After Spence had relayed what Rick had noticed, they were on their way to Premium Point to look around.

The drive took roughly fifteen minutes, and when they reached the private community, they were screened by a guard.

"This is the kind of neighborhood where it's not likely a stranger could go unseen," Spence stated.

"She either came out or was taken out by someone she knows."

"Is that the ocean?" Rick asked.

"The Long Island Sound. An estuary of the Atlantic Ocean."

"Across the way is Long Island," Gunner added.

"The staff could move rather freely without notice," Fletch said.

"Good point."

They continued down the tree-lined road in their rented black four-door SUV. Rick couldn't help but stare at the mansions they drove by. Arthur, who had saved him all those years ago, had a house as big as these in Lincoln Park, Chicago. It felt like a lifetime ago.

Gunner slowed the SUV before turning into a laneway that snaked across pristinely cut grass and topiaries. In the distance, he could see the roof of a building that grew in size the closer they got. The laneway changed from concrete to cut stone when they got within fifty yards of the house. A four-car garage stood off to the right while the three-story brick mansion stood to the left.

Rick wasn't impressed, and by the looks on the others' faces, neither were they.

"This place would be a bitch to heat," Fletch said. "Can you imagine the water bill?"

"If you're living here, you don't have to worry about those things," Spence said. "Why would one family of three people need all this?"

"Because they can," Rick answered, his tone as cold as the rock slabs surrounding the gardens.

Spence's phone beeped, and he looked at the screen before smiling wide. "Looks like there's more than talk about this tell-all. There's a signed contract."

"Who is it?"

"The publisher is Wade and Senss out of California, but no one seems to know who was supplying the information for the book."

"Holy shit. The Hammons' secrets won't remain that way for long."

"Couldn't happen to a nicer couple," Rick said, unashamed of his happiness.

"Agreed."

Gunner parked near the front door, and they got out. Fletch and Gunner would take the grounds while he and Spence took a look around inside. It felt strange being part of the team, considering he'd never imagined it would happen. Generally, he wasn't well-liked by the team, but he shuffled that away for now. Ellen must be found.

Spence pushed the doorbell and pulled his finger away as if he'd been burned.

"Are you okay?"

"Yeah, it was only a shock."

The thick front door creaked open, revealing a woman wearing a black uniform with a white apron. "Hello, I'm Marie. We've been expecting you, L. H. Investigations."

"You might want to get your doorbell fixed." Rick had to mention it in case they didn't know.

"Oh no, did it shock you? I've had the repairman out twice now to fix it. It began two weeks ago. I'm so sorry." Rick was a bit surprised by the woman's authenticity. She truly appeared to be contrite. "Come in. Can I get you anything for your finger?"

"No. It surprised me, but the sting is fading, thank you. We're here to look around and ask a few questions to aid us in finding Ellen."

"Yes. Please make yourselves at home. You can call me on the phone's paging system if you need something, just dial nine."

"Thank you, Marie."

She nodded and walked down the hall. They had a general map of the house in the file, which would help them get through the maze of rooms.

"Let's start with Ellen's room," Spence suggested.

Spence led the way, and Rick followed, taking in his surroundings. Art, decorative but not "important," hung with the lighting perfectly set, a vase under glass that would never hold a flower, and chandeliers hung in various sizes and shapes, sending sparkling light across the rooms.

They went by a theater room that could hold at least twelve people, and an empty gym sat at the ready with the latest in equipment, though he doubted they'd seen a drop of sweat. Hallways veered off in all directions, and every inch of the home was *Architectural Digest* ready. The house was like some people he used to know, stunning in appearance but lacking a heart and soul.

"This place is a museum, not a home," Spence said as they turned a corner.

"Or a morgue. It's so white and creamy in here."

The place lacked color, with tones in white and beige being the chosen aesthetic, making him wonder even more about Ellen's room filled with colorful belongings. Did the young girl like color, or was it a direct result of having none elsewhere in her home? More questions without answers. This missing person's case was taking so many turns it might as well be a ride at the county fair.

"Here it is," Spence announced as they neared a closed door. "I want you to open the door and get a feel for it."

"Do you mean what Ellen was trying to say?"

"Exactly."

Rick reached for the handle and slowly opened the door. The shock of color was an assault on his senses, especially after coming through the rest of the house. The contrast was enough to make him step back.

"Get out," Rick said.

"What?" Spence asked.

"She's screaming at her parents to stay out. Ellen made her room into a bomb shelter of sorts where she could go when things became too much. I get the bright colors now that I've seen other parts of the house. It would be so jarring to what her parents were going for or wanted I doubt they went in here."

"Shit. What kinda life did she have if she fought back with bright, happy colors?"

"Your case is getting stranger by the minute."

"Mine? This sucker is yours as well. You want to find Ellen as much as we do."

Instead of answering, Rick walked into the room. He didn't know what he thought about being considered part of the team, so he kept his mouth shut.

He felt as if he was trespassing in someone's safe place, and he knew what it felt like to have that done to him. He kept reminding himself that this was needed to find Ellen, or he would've backed out immediately.

Spence knelt beside the bed to look underneath, and something must've caught his eye because soon enough, he was on his back, sliding under.

"See something?"

"Yeah," Spence said. "A small box tucked under a bed rail."

When he came out, he handed the box to Rick before he stood. It was only a few inches long and looked like an old matchbox. Maybe Ellen was taking drugs.

When he slid it open, Rick's world began to spin, and he knew he was headed for the floor.

# CHAPTER TWELVE

*Spence*

Rick's face went white, and Spence caught him before he collapsed to the floor. He held him close while retrieving the box from his shaking hand before sitting Rick on the bed.

"You okay?" His reaction was so sudden.

"Sorry, I wasn't expecting to see that."

Spence placed the box out of Rick's view before opening it. Inside sat two razor blades, both stained with blood.

"She was cutting herself," Rick explained. "When your life isn't under your control, you do anything to feel powerful again."

"Did you?" Spence asked, feeling an ugly weight settle in his stomach.

"Oh yeah. On the inside of my thighs. It started when my dad moved us to Chicago and escalated from there."

Spence pulled Rick in close. "You've been through hell, sweetheart."

"And so has this girl. We need to find her. Now." Rick's look said it all: he trusted Spence to do the right thing.

"We will," Spence swore while placing the box on the top of the dresser. "Do you need to leave? I'll help you out."

"No way. Somebody has to know where Ellen is, and I'm not stopping 'til we find her. She'll never have to come back here again." Rick sat up straight and sucked in a deep breath before standing. "Let's keep looking."

Spence was in awe of Rick's strength. No matter how hard life hit him, he stood back up and carried on. His slender stature made little difference to the size of the spirit in the man, and Spence wanted to be near him. To hold him.

Simon didn't know the hell he'd brought down on his head, but he'd soon find out.

Rick turned to look at Spence with a strange expression on his face. "My real name is Adam Jefferson."

Spence was speechless. Rick had given them information on Simon and his location but stopped short of telling them his birth name. That he now trusted Spence with this information, he took seriously.

"Thank you for telling me."

"I wanted you to know the real me," Rick said before standing and walking over to a desk at the far end of the room. "Aside from Roman, you are the only other person in my new life to know."

Spence got the hint Rick needed space while owning his truth: the distance while he continued searching gave Rick a buffer from the intensity of what he'd shared.

Spence had been attracted to the man since the first time they met and grew to respect him over the past year for his strength and his need to care for others. Now that respect deepened, and added to it was adoration for the man he'd made himself into.

Even now, with Simon hunting him, Rick was doing everything in his power to find Ellen without thought of himself. Spence felt privileged to know him by whichever name he chose.

He zeroed back onto the case and went to the dresser that had the mark on the wall beside it. Carefully pulling out the drawers, Spence searched for hidden compartments, writing, or further clues about who Ellen Hammon truly was. Perfect images crack eventually, and he couldn't imagine the stress on this young girl to keep up. The cutting might be the tip of the iceberg.

After taking out all five drawers, Spence noticed slight indents and tiny holes on the thin back panel as if something had been pressed against it from the other side. He lifted one end of the dresser and pulled it away from the wall.

*Shit.*

"Rick, you should have a look at this."

"Whatcha find?" Rick asked as he came up beside Spence. By Rick's deep intake of breath, Spence figured no answer was needed. "Oh."

There, on the back of her dresser, Ellen had drawn a family tree of sorts on the thin piece of wood. Spence took out his phone and began taking pictures while Rick looked closer. The first two people at the top were Commander Rask and his second wife, June. Then arrows led down their daughter, Elise: Ellen's mother. After that, things got a bit strange.

There were two vertical lines drawn from Elise, one was to Ellen, and the other was without a name indicating she'd had a second child. Another line was drawn horizontally to a blank spot and then another to Tom Hammon. Under Tom, she'd written "Boy 2003," and under the blank spot, a line circled back to Ellen's name.

"I guess we have our answer; Ellen knew Tom wasn't her biological father, and that Tom had a son."

"I wonder if that came as a relief considering how he must've treated her, plus knowing her real father was out there."

"Not to mention, it appears Elise has two children, not the one as she claimed."

"Could the other child have passed away, and that's why they haven't said anything?"

"No. When I did a background check, there was only one registered birth under Elise's name."

They looked back at the drawing, and Spence noticed something missing. "Look. This small hole suggests a thumbtack was used here to hold something."

Spence got down on his knees and looked under the other end of the dresser. Sure enough, a bright pink thumbtack lay on the ground underneath. He stood and lifted the entire piece of furniture to the middle of the room.

The bright pink thumbtack sat on the carpeted floor, reminding Spence of Poe's beating heart underneath the floorboards. It still had a small piece of paper attached, and when Rick bent to retrieve it, Spence was quick to stop him.

"Stop. Don't touch that," he yelled, causing Rick to jump back as if he'd been burned.

Spence went over and wrapped his arm around him. "Sorry, but if there's DNA or fingerprints, we don't want to mess with the evidence."

"Oh, I didn't even think of that. You're right. I'll keep it in mind from this point forward."

"Good," Spence said, squeezing him before stepping toward a scrap of paper and taking a picture. "Actually, my fault. We should've worn nitrile gloves." He pulled out a small plastic bag from his jacket pocket and turned the paper over using a paper clip from the desk. There were letters, the tail ends of two words where the page had been ripped, and the tip of an emblem Spence knew well. The rope around the seal of the United States Navy. "Things have taken a turn," Spence announced.

"For the good?" Rick asked.

"No. Why would a teenage girl have something relating to the Navy pinned to the back of her dresser?"

"Do you think Rask is involved?" Rick asked. It made sense.

"If he is, he's one of the best liars I've ever met. I didn't get a single vibe that he knew where his granddaughter was."

"Maybe he's involved but has nothing to do with Ellen's disappearance."

"Good point. Either way, we need to get it dusted to see if we have any useable prints or a partial to go on."

Spence nudged the paper and tack into the plastic bag and sealed it before they searched the rest of the room, but unfortunately found nothing else of use. Spence pulled out his cell phone and dialed Fletch.

"Hey man, find anything outside?"

"No, but I had a thought. We're close enough to open water for someone to've used it as a means of escape if Ellen was kidnapped. The front guard would've never known."

"Then what would be the sense of saying she disappeared on her way to school?"

"Big shock. Someone's lying," Fletch huffed.

"When you guys are done, I want you to grab the fingerprint kit from the case in the back of the SUV. There's a dresser we need dusted for prints. I'll run the fingerprints when we get back to the rental."

"On it."

Spence turned around to find Rick staring at him. "What's wrong?"

"You guys can do anything."

"I don't know about that."

"Your team has the power to find things no one else is looking for. You have the intelligence and tools to find the answers and the strength to see it through to the end. That's amazing, and I hadn't realized it until right now."

"We've trained for decades to prepare for any possibility and ensure we have the equipment to do the job."

"Have you looked into me?"

"No. Other than to confirm you weren't the one attacking Roman last year."

Rick's head cocked to the side. "Why?"

"It didn't feel right. I wanted you to tell me about yourself, and I didn't want to invade your privacy."

"That must've been tough to resist because I never would've known."

"I would," Spence stated.

Rick continued to stare at him, and Spence didn't know what else to say, so he waited.

The handsome man who'd starred in many of Spence's dreams stepped closer and said, "Thank you."

"You're welcome," was all he managed to say before Fletch walked into the room.

He took one look at them and said, "I can come back."

"No. We need to move as quickly as possible on this," Spence said. "Let's go have a word with the staff. Where's Gunner?"

"Still looking around the property. This place is massive."

Spence slid the plastic evidence bag back into his jacket pocket, grabbed Rick's hand, and led him out of the room. He stopped when they were alone in the hallway and pressed Rick against the wall.

"I want to make one thing clear. You and I are far from done." He leaned in and took Rick's lips into a punishing kiss that had him moaning.

Rick's hands traveled up Spence's chest, then he wrapped his arms around Spence's neck. He had to slow the kiss too soon, and at Rick's confused look, he said, "Case first."

Nodding, Rick agreed. "Right."

***

*Rick*

Rick's head was still spinning when they walked into the stark white kitchen where the three staff were waiting for them. He'd dissect what just happened when he was alone in his room.

Marie and Joe stood around the kitchen island drinking coffee while Rita added more salt to whatever was cooking in the pot on the gas stove.

"Good morning, everyone. We met Marie on our way in, so that leaves Rita and Joe," Spence said as both people nodded their heads. "Great, let's get started. Where is Ellen?"

Rick loved how Spence went straight for the jugular. No warm-up, no nothing.

All three glanced back and forth, but Marie was the one to answer while the other two shook their heads. "We don't know."

And the questioning began.

Joe reminded Rick of Tom, and he guessed him to be in his forties. All he'd have to do is look in the file to find out, but instead of concentrating on their words, Rick preferred to watch the expressions on their faces and look for little signs that gave them away. Most people had *tells* or movements that gave away their real intentions or thoughts when they were nervous, scared, or lying.

For example, Rita turned her attention to her cooking every time a question was asked, avoiding answering any questions. She'd already added salt to the boiling mixture three times without tasting it once. No cook would do that, and when she tasted whatever it was, she couldn't hide her grimace.

Joe stood as still as stone. His coffee cup cradled between his hands, staring straight at Spence. Marie continued to answer the questions as the muscles in Joe's jaw gave away his clenched teeth, as if he was desperately trying to stay quiet.

As for Marie, she was friendly and open. Smiled often and answered every question asked with complete answers as if they'd been practiced.

"What are your hours of work?"

Marie piped up again. "Usually seven am until seven pm unless they have an event."

"All of you?" Spence pointedly asked the other two.

"Yes," Marie answered.

Enough was enough, and Spence was getting frustrated with their canned answers.

"Okay, either you tell me what's going on, or I'll drag you into the station and have you questioned separately," Spence warned, crossing his sizeable arms.

The fear was instant. "No. No station, please," Rita said as she broke her silence.

"You can't take her to the police station," Joe quickly joined in and wrapped a protective arm around Rita.

"Why?"

Rita looked between Joe and Marie as tears began streaming from her eyes. "I'm not in this country legally."

Rick felt a weight being lifted. "Is this what the three of you are so afraid of?"

"Yes. I'm legal because I was born here," Marie explained. "My mother would be sent back into a war zone."

Spence uncrossed his arms and visibly relaxed. "We're not going to report your mom to border agents. All we want is to find Ellen."

"Can you help us do that, please?" Rick asked, hoping they knew something.

Joe set down his coffee and said, "Okay."

"What do you know about her disappearance?" Spence asked.

Rita shut off the stove, and Rick couldn't help himself. "What are you cooking?"

"It was supposed to be a marinara sauce."

"Too salty."

Rita smiled. "You could say that."

Rick laughed, and Rita smiled as the stress in the room faded, and they all went to sit around the marble kitchen table.

"How are things around here with the family?" Rick asked.

"Strange," Marie answered.

"Dysfunctional," Joe said.

"Sad," Rita whispered, catching Rick's attention.

"Why sad?"

"There was no love or family in this house. Three individuals were cohabitating," she explained. "Ellen didn't have a chance."

"The Hammons' parenting style leaves a lot to be desired," Marie agreed. "Ellen stayed in her room mainly when her parents were home. I'd bring her meals there."

"They were cold and barely spoke unless they had company, and then they were the loving hosts and the life of the party."

"Were all three of you here the morning Ellen disappeared?"

"Yes, though Joe was in the garage working on one of the Hammons' cars when Ellen came in for breakfast."

"She had her usual backpack with her and her laptop, and she ate her cheese omelet here on the island instead of the table."

"How was she behaving?"

"Over the last couple of months, she's been different, more removed from the family."

"Couple months? Since her grandmother died?"

Marie looked at the others before answering. "I believe so. Ellen loved her grandmother. She was the only family member Ellen was close to."

"Did she visit with Ellen often?"

"Yes. Quite regularly."

"What happened after Ellen ate her breakfast?"

"She ran to her bedroom to grab something, gathered her things, and left for the bus stop."

"Bus stop? Why didn't you drive her to school?" Rick asked Joe.

"I was covered in oil at the time."

"Where's the bus stop?"

"Outside the gates to the north."

Rick remembered the drive from the front gate to the house was short, but it would still take at least fifteen minutes to walk that far. Had someone been waiting for her?

"Did she take the bus often?" Rick asked.

"No. Usually, I drive her, but Mr. Hammon called and demanded I change the oil in all their vehicles immediately that morning."

"Did he do things like that often, where he'd put in a last-minute request and tell you to do it right away?" Spence asked.

"No, not really. I have a monthly calendar of chores and repairs. He's not in the habit of asking me to deviate from it."

Spence took notes on his iPad, and Rick could tell something about Joe's answer bugged him.

"Can I see this calendar?" Spence asked.

"Sure," Joe answered as he stood and walked over to the pantry. He had a wall calendar in his hand when he came back. "This is for the last six months."

Spence took the calendar and flipped through the pages before handing it to Rick. He looked through the months and found a repeated schedule of maintenance that didn't vary much from month to month.

Alarm bells started sounding in Rick's mind. Why would Tom call to have the work done knowing Ellen needed to be driven to school? The "spontaneous" request made him look involved in her disappearance.

"When was Ellen informed she'd be walking?" Rick asked.

"When she came down for breakfast that morning," Rita answered.

"Do you know why Rosaline, Ellen's nanny, was fired so suddenly?" Spence asked.

"I suspect it was because Ellen had called Rosaline 'mom' in front of Mrs. Hammon," Marie answered.

"I remember that morning," Rita said. "Ellen was on her way out the door to school when she said, 'See ya, Mom,' and kissed Rosaline on the cheek. Elise was sitting at the kitchen table, and as soon as Ellen left, she told Rosaline she would no longer be needed. She was crying as she packed her belongings."

"Ouch. But no one could blame Ellen for feeling closer to her nanny than her uninvolved mother," Rick stated.

"Do you know where we can find Rosaline?" Spence asked.

"I did a few years ago. We fell out of touch," Marie said. "I'll write it down for you."

"Thank you."

They continued with the questioning, but nothing else that was said stuck out as damning as Tom's request.

# CHAPTER THIRTEEN
*Spence*

Spence read the email twice to make sure he wasn't seeing things. June Rask DOA from an overdose of fentanyl. He'd looked into Ellen's grandmother, and she was as normal as a person could be, other than her extensive bone china doll collection. She went to church regularly, participated in local charities and food drives, and volunteered at the local animal shelter. Nothing that screamed drug user.

According to her medical records, June hadn't been prescribed the medication by her doctor, and previous physicals reported nothing odd in her blood samples. As far as friends, they were all shocked when June died. She'd been healthy and an active part of the community until she was found dead in her home.

All the evidence led Spence to an obvious conclusion. June Rask was murdered.

"Shit. Things have gotten well past Ellen running away. And it looks like we can take her being carried away by boat off the board. The staff said she left the house from the front to walk to the bus stop."

Gunner, Fletch, and Rick looked over from the whiteboard they were using to keep the information straight. The family tree Ellen had created was on the left, and on the other side was a list of all the active players. Rask, Tom, Elise, Susan Stapleton, their manager, Dylan, Tom's love child, and the staff at the morning show. They had a meeting with them scheduled for four that afternoon.

Jacob and the house staff were taken off the list. Tom was the person of interest given his out-of-character request, which put Ellen in the unusual position of having to walk to the bus stop.

"What do you know we don't?"

"June Rask died of an overdose."

"Oh no, that's sad," Rick said.

"Any history of drug use?" Fletch asked.

"None."

"Was she acting erratically?" Gunner asked.

"Friends and neighbors were shocked, never saw it coming. Plus, there's no record of a prescription for fentanyl or any other painkiller."

"Odds are someone planned her demise," Fletch said.

"Planned?" Rick asked.

"Murder. Covered up as a drug overdose," Spence answered.

"Damn, our missing person's case has turned into a murder case." Rick rubbed his forehead.

"Yeah, it totally has."

\*\*\*

*Morning Show Boardroom*

*Rick*

The room was filled with people, and a few looked pissed about being there. Susan, the Hammons' manager, was one of them.

"Okay, quiet down," John, the morning show producer, said from the end of the table. "These gentlemen are here to ask questions regarding the disappearance of Ellen Hammon."

"We've already done this with the cops," a tall man in a three-piece suit grumbled.

Gunner looked through the files. "Thanks for speaking up, Jerome Thornberry, station weatherman. We'll start with you. Follow me."

"Meteorologist," Jerome growled, threw his hands in the air, and stood. "Anything to get out of here."

He followed Gunner out. Each person was going to be questioned separately. SOP when dealing with a group of people who probably talked to get their story straight.

"I'll take Susan Stapleton," Fletcher stated. "Follow me."

One by one, each person, from lighting to makeup, had been questioned, and, as it turned out, Susan's contract managing the Hammons wasn't being renewed. Also, the makeup artist mentioned several staff members were looking for new jobs. Rick sat through a few interviews, taking notes, but no one piqued his interest.

They were down to the final two interviews, the cameraman and the producer. Rick went with the cameraman, Donald Speirs. Something about the guy, including he was the local government conspiracist and UFO hunter, made Rick curious. If anyone had their hand on the heartbeat of this place, it would be that guy.

Rick followed Fletcher and Donald into a separate room while Spence and Gunner took the producer. The office they walked into had a table and chairs but little else, suggesting it was a spare and belonged to no one.

Donald's faded red baseball cap had started fraying around the brim, and Rick guessed he'd had it for a long time. He was thirty-six years old and single, still living at home in his mother's basement. His shoes were orthopedic, and he had a wrist guard on his right hand like those typically used by carpel tunnel sufferers. His cell phone was attached to a clip on his belt, and he wore a medical alert bracelet.

"Have a seat, Mr. Speirs," Fletch instructed, and the man sat.

Rick decided to try a different approach, and when Fletch looked over at him and nodded, he began.

"Donald, let's cut to the chase. We know you didn't have anything to do with Ellen's disappearance." The guy's scruffy eyebrows shot up, but Rick continued before he could say anything. "However, I believe you can be an asset to us."

"An asset?" Donald asked, unable to contain his smile. "You mean like work for you."

"More of an unpaid consultant, if you may. I've worked with men like you. Nothing happens around here without you knowing about it." Rick added a healthy dose of respect to his voice.

Donald's smile widened. "I like to think I keep an eye on things. Are you guys working for the government?"

"No. Private investigations company hired to find Ellen. But there's more going on here than that. Isn't there?"

Donald did the classic glance around the room as if someone would pop out of the wall. When he was satisfied they were alone, Donald said, "Oh yeah."

"That's what I thought," Rick said. Now it was time to schmooze a bit. "Men like you aren't satisfied with the run-of-the-mill answers. You find your own truths. I respect that."

Donald sat a bit straighter in his seat. "It's nice somebody finally notices."

"It takes one to know one, my friend." Rick figured he'd get more and better responses if Donald believed he was talking to a compadre.

"Susan's going to sue Elise and Tom for getting rid of her at the end of their contract," he said. "I heard her talking to a lawyer. Oh, and John's sleeping with Elise."

"The producer of the morning show?" Gunner asked.

"The one and same. It's been going on for years, and Tom doesn't care because he's making unbelievable amounts of money in endorsements as long as they appear to be a happy family."

"Really?" Rick dragged out the word, playing along even though they knew the Hammons' marriage was a sham.

"Absolutely." Donald's eyes got big as he nodded. "I've caught them making out in his office."

"So, what do you think is going on around here?" Fletcher asked as he leaned against the table.

The guy looked over at Rick, who nodded for Donald to spill the tea.

Donald leaned into the table as if he didn't want to speak too loudly. "I saw two men leading Tom away from his car in the parking lot."

That was new information. "When was this?" Rick asked.

"Thirty-eight days ago, three-thirty-six pm."

"Did you recognize the men?" Fletch asked as tapped in a few notes to his iPad.

"No, but they looked official. If you know what I mean."

"Military?"

Donald tapped the side of his nose and leaned back in his chair like a character in one of those old-time detective movies.

"Did Tom look like he knew these men?" Rick asked.

"No, and by their locked arms, it didn't look like he had much choice."

Fletch leaned in a little more. "Did you see these men again?"

"Yeah. I saw them in John's office three days later, and he didn't look all that happy either."

"The producer?" Rick wanted to be clear.

"The very one. And now that I think about it, starting about the same time, I haven't seen Elise leaving for her normal long lunch."

"Long lunch? You mean hooking up with John?" Fletch asked.

"Yeah."

"How old would you say these men were?" Fletch continued.

"Both had graying hair, and one walked with a slight limp as if he were favoring his right leg, so I'm guessing early sixties."

Rick knew the guy missed nothing. He understood what drove people like that to want control over their surroundings. "Is there anything else you've found odd going on around the station?"

"Neither Elise nor Tom have any family photos in their offices. It was like Ellen didn't exist until it was convenient to pull her out like a pet, but it didn't help their ratings this time around."

"What about their ratings?" Rick knew numbers drove "talent's" success and stickability in a job.

"The ratings for the morning show have been tanking over the last eight months because a newer, fresher morning talk show from another station is pulling their fans away. They were bored with the same old, same old."

"How have the ratings been since Ellen went missing?"

"Better than the last decade's worth of ratings. It was like people couldn't get enough of their story."

They asked a few more questions that didn't give them anything they didn't know. "Thanks for all your help. I want to give you my number and email if you think of anything else." Rick wrote his number on a scrap piece of paper he pulled from his pocket and handed it to the guy. "One more thing. I'm curious, have you ever heard of the NOAH Project?" It was a long shot, but they had nothing to lose. Spence, who could find anything that had been written down anywhere, wasn't turning up anything.

"No, but I can ask around to some of my friends and associates."

"It's more than we could hope for."

Again, Donald sat straighter in his chair. "I'll be in touch."

# CHAPTER FOURTEEN

*Spence*

At two in the morning, another damn nightmare woke Spence. His PTSD had a field day torturing him, and he couldn't escape to his island. Instead, he lay in bed staring at the popcorn ceiling. He decided to work and had grabbed his laptop from downstairs, but had yet to turn it on.

Though his nightmare remained the same, the severity had increased over the past six months, and Spence knew he'd eventually have to go to therapy. There was nothing wrong with therapy, but sitting around talking about his feelings sounded too much like more, unnecessary torture.

His nightmare was filled with exploding ordinance, and he was forced to watch as soldier after soldier was blown apart by the blasts. Good men and women who had been offering aid. It was an impossible situation.

Earlier, he'd received a report from Brick: he and Shaw were tracking down Simon in Chicago. So far, they'd gotten as far as the Rogers Park area, but had yet to find the guy. Spence didn't doubt they'd find him, but he'd feel a hell of a lot better once they had.

Research on the guy had yielded a long, illustrious history of crime. However, Simon hadn't been convicted of anything that netted him serious time. His lackeys took the fall, while he'd gotten a slap on the wrist.

A soft knock on his door had Spence sitting up. Who the hell would want to speak with him at this hour? "Come in," he grumbled.

His bedroom door opened to reveal the last person he expected to walk in.

"Are you okay, Rick?" Spence climbed out of bed to join him by the door, thankful he'd kept his shorts on.

"Yeah, I'm good. I heard you get up a little bit ago and wondered if you were working."

Rick was wearing a pair of long shorts and a t-shirt, but the fact that he had his arms wrapped around himself was telling.

"I was thinking about researching the show a bit more. Are you cold?"

"No. You can't sleep?"

"On and off. My brain isn't giving me any peace tonight."

"Nightmares?"

At Spence's nod, Rick said, "Me too. Do you mind if I lie down with you to see if that helps?" Rick looked exhausted. "His face keeps crashing my dreams."

"Simon?"

"Yeah."

"Sure. I promise you'll be perfectly safe." He'd watch over the man all night.

"I know. That's why I asked." Rick gave him a small smile.

Spence's heart skipped a beat. Trust was hard to earn, and he'd do nothing to betray what it had to've taken Rick a lot to ask. Spence waited until Rick chose which side he wanted to sleep on. It didn't matter to Spence since he usually slept right in the middle of the mattress.

He pulled back the covers, and Rick curled into the right side, so Spence went left. After they sorted out the blankets, he had one burning question, and he hoped Rick wouldn't say no.

"Can I hold you?"

"I wish you would," Rick said, his voice scratchy and tired.

"You got it."

Spence moved closer and pulled Rick into the curve of his body until they were spooning. Rick's blond hair tickled Spence's cheek, but there was no way in hell he was going to change positions. This was where he wanted to be, and not only for one night.

Admitting that surprised him, but it was a truth he'd known in his heart for a while. If Rick would give him a chance, he'd never do anything to make him regret it.

"Comfortable?"

"Oh yeah. This is perfect," Rick mumbled before snuggling deeper. "And warm."

"Yeah."

It wasn't long before Rick's breathing evened out, and Spence's chest swelled with satisfaction. He lay there listening to Rick's breathing for a long time, and the last thing he remembered was wrapping his leg over the top of Rick's legs, using his body to cover most of Rick's. He'd do anything to ensure nothing could reach him. Blessed sleep followed, and it was sorely needed.

When Spence woke, he felt more rested than he had in years. He slowly opened his eyes and saw a pair of bright blue eyes looking up at him. Warmth filled him, and he pulled Rick even closer to his body.

"How'd you sleep?"

"Better than I have in a long, long time. Thanks for letting me to stay here with you." Rick stretched out his lithe body, rubbing himself against Spence.

"You don't have to thank me. You're welcome to join me anytime."

"Did you get back to sleep?

"Totally. Best I've had in recent memory." The admission came easily. Apparently, he didn't mind sharing with Rick. "I didn't have one nightmare while I was holding you." It'd been forever since he'd been able to say that.

"Same. Logically that means we should continue with this experiment to make sure it wasn't an anomaly."

"Agreed. Same place tonight?"

"No, let's change it up," Rick said with a wicked smile. "We'll sleep in my room."

Spence couldn't help but smile back. Unable to stop himself, he leaned down and licked Rick's pouty lower lip before kissing him until they were both breathless. Rick's moans and gasps drove Spence crazy, and he pulled him so close, there wasn't space between them.

The silky glide of their lips as they explored each other's mouths had caused other parts of his body to perk up and take notice. Rick's hands worked their way down his chest and over his abs, sending chills of excitement through his body. All he wanted was in his arms, and he made a promise to himself not to mess it up.

"Is this okay?" Spence asked.

Rick's smile was instant. "Yeah. Don't stop."

So he didn't. He removed Rick's t-shirt so they could be skin to skin.

"You're so warm," Rick said as he nuzzled Spence's neck.

"Hot-blooded Italian through and through." He laughed before diving in for another kiss. Rick responded by rubbing his hard cock against Spence's. Spence had no desire to hide how he was feeling, and he reciprocated Rick's movements.

Rick's hands ghosted down his back, causing Spence's heart to speed up in anticipation, but Rick stopped on his clothed butt cheeks and gave a squeeze.

"You've got a sexy ass," Rick said when they finally came up for air.

"Do I?"

"Hell yeah. Have you ever used a full-length mirror? Your glutes are tight, and I want to take a bite out of them."

Spence couldn't help but laugh. "You're crazy, and sexy too. That's a couple of reasons why I'm falling for you."

"You're falling for me?"

"Oh yeah, completely."

"What if I'm not what you need?"

"You're everything I need."

"But I'm nothing. A former prostitute who has a psycho after him."

"You're not nothing," Spence growled. "It pisses me off when you sell yourself short. And what does it say about me since you're the man I'm crazy about? Do I need to give you a list of your qualities? You have to know how you go out of your way to help and care for others, putting the people you care about before yourself. You're good and kind, and when I hold you, you make me feel better about myself, especially after everything I've done."

Rick stared at him, before he stuttered, "You...you th-think that about me?"

"Totally."

"Um. Thanks?" Rick was quiet for a few moments before his gaze started wandering over Spence's body. "What does this tattoo say?" He pointed at the large tattoo on Spence's right forearm.

"It's a poem by William Ernest Henley named *Invictus.*"

"Can I read it?" Rick asked.

"Sure," Spence said as he stretched out his arm for Rick to see. He read it aloud.

*Out of the night that covers me,*
*Black as the pit from pole to pole,*
*I thank whatever gods may be*
*For my unconquerable soul.*
*In the fell clutch of circumstance*
*I have not winced nor cried aloud.*
*Under the bludgeonings of chance*
*My head is bloody but unbowed.*
*Beyond this place of wrath and tears*
*Looms but the Horror of the shade,*
*And yet the menace of the years*
*Finds and shall find me unafraid.*
*It matters not how strait the gate,*

*How charged with punishments the scroll,*
*I am the master of my fate,*
*I am the captain of my soul.*

Before Spence could say a word or lean in to kiss Rick, the perimeter alarms sounded. "Shit. You stay here," Spence ordered as he jumped from the bed, slid his jeans over his hard-on, and grabbed his Glock. "You'll be safe while we go check this out." He waited for Rick to nod, then said, "Don't leave this room."

Talk about bad timing. The universe was screwing with him because something happened every time they got close. A phone call, people walking in, alarms sounding.

He stepped out the bedroom and waited until he heard the door's lock engaged. Taking the stairs two at a time, he arrived in the kitchen at the same time Gunner dragged an unidentified man into the living room through the patio door. The sun hadn't risen yet, but the sky was light.

"Who the hell is this?"

"He says his name is Conor O'Brian," Fletcher snapped as he walked in behind Gunner.

*Why does that name seem familiar?*

"You know the guy whose license you had revoked permanently," the man growled.

"You're the PI asshole who's been following Gunner," Spence stated. "You helped that bastard try to take his nephew away from his legal guardian."

"After what the family has said, Ben would be better off with them. All-night parties, women, drugs. That's bullshit, and you know it."

"Parties?" Gunner asked. "Women? You fell for a pile of bullshit, bub."

"You were played, dude." Fletcher chuckled. "It appears quite easily, which is probably one of the reasons why your license got pulled in the first place."

"Don't give me that shit. You know what I'm talking about," the idiot said, holding to his position.

"Women?" Rick's voice came from the staircase. *Goddammit. He didn't listen again.* "But Gunner's gay," Rick stated.

"You've been fed a load, you imbecile," Fletcher snarled.

"Yeah, right. I don't give a rat's ass. All I want is for you guys to undo what you did."

"You don't care you help a man who's more interested in my sister's life insurance than his grandson. My sister made me his legal guardian, and no matter how many lies those fuckers think up, they will not get Ben."

Spence noticed the confusion in Conor's eyes before covering it with indifference.

"Maybe you should've done a few background checks before taking the job," Spence suggested.

"I'm hired to find people. It's what I do."

"Did you ever think about using your talents to help people, decent people who are missing?" Rick asked, and there he went trying to help. He couldn't stop himself.

"I have bills to pay, and I take jobs I can do. Will you undo what you did to my license?"

"I can," Spence said. "But the question is: should I undo it?"

"I won't be coming near Gunner and Ben again. You have my word."

Spence glanced at Gunner. This was his call. With a slight nod, he knew what he had to do.

"Okay, asshole. If I get one whiff of you skulking around Gunner and his nephew, all bets are off, and I will erase you from existence."

Conor's eyes widened. "Are you threatening to kill me?"

"No," Rick said. "Bit of a drama queen, aren't you? He meant that any record of you and your life would be wiped clean."

"Who are you guys?"

"That's confidential. Now get the fuck out and stay gone, you parasite." Fletcher pointed to the front door. "Don't ever think about coming near any of us again."

Conor looked around at the men with a shrewd eye before turning and walking out the front door. Fletch slammed it shut behind him with more force than necessary, shaking the pictures on the wall.

Spence turned to Rick, who moved to his side. "I thought I told you to stay up in my room until everything was clear."

Rick leaned into Spence before saying, "You should know better than that."

"I told you don't move for a reason. What if it had been Simon?"

"Then I'm positive you, Fletch, and Gunner would've protected me." Rick turned and wrapped his arms around Spence's waist. The intimacy of that move wasn't lost on him, and Spence pulled him closer in return.

"That's not the right answer. We could've prevented him from getting anywhere near you if you hadn't come downstairs. You have to trust us to do our jobs."

"When will this shit end?" Gunner huffed. "Ben is settling and is finally smiling again, and now grandparents he's never been close to are trying to ruin that."

Rick released Spence and walked over to Gunner. He grabbed his upper arms and said, "We'll do whatever it takes to stop that from happening. I swear it."

Spence glanced over at Fletch, who was watching closely.

"Um." Fletch blew out a puff of breath, then shook his head. "I've behaved like a complete asshole to you, Rick, and I'm sorry."

Gunner looked down at Rick and nodded. "Ditto."

Rick released Gunner and went over to Fletcher, who slapped Rick on the back. Spence was pleased they saw the real Rick.

"It's okay, you redheaded beast."

Rick used the same name he always called Fletch, though this time it was with affection and not in anger.

"Can I ask about the special diet you put us on? Is there room for changes?"

"Of course there is."

"Thank you, thank you." Fletch slapped him on the back again, making Rick bow forward. "What got you into the health food kick? Were you raised like that?"

"No. An angel of a man named Arthur, whom I cared for deeply, died from heart disease. After that, fear for my health and everyone I care about's health motivated me."

"You were afraid one of us would die?" Gunner asked.

Rick shrugged. "Pretty stupid, right?"

"No, it's not," Fletch said. "I get why, and it's not a bad thing. You're a bit intense about it, but I get it."

"Who was Arthur?" Gunner asked.

"The man who saved me from Simon when I was nothing but a street rat. He saw something in me, and it had nothing to do with sex. I guess you could say, Arthur took me in and cleaned me up."

"Did Simon come looking for you?" Spence asked.

"Oh yeah. Immediately. But it turned out Arthur was better connected than Simon could ever hope to be, and he was forced to back off. I spent three years happily by that man's side, learning, traveling, keeping him company, and he never asked me for a thing. When he started to get sick, and his heart began failing, he sent me away so Simon couldn't find me. He died two weeks after I left." Tears ran down Rick's face, and Spence understood Rick had loved that man for what he'd done to save him. Of course, he'd never forget him.

Spence pulled Rick into his arms and held him close. He owed this Arthur a debt of gratitude for saving Rick. "Is that how you managed to meet up with Roman?"

Rick nodded as he wiped his eyes on his shirt sleeve. "Once I got over the initial grief of losing Arthur, I used the tools he'd provided me to create my new life free from anyone's ownership."

Spence continued to hold Rick tight and caught Gunner's and Fletch's stares.

They were touched by what Rick had revealed, and they would make sure Rick stayed safe and free.

# CHAPTER FIFTEEN
*Spence*

"Great way to start the day," Spence growled as he looked down at the body of the Morning Show's cameraman who had given them the inside scoop on what was going on around here. Poor Donald. "Someone wants to keep the lid on what's going on here."

Rick stood behind him, unable to look at the man they'd questioned the day before. He'd been stuffed into a Dumpster behind the television station, clearly a warning to anyone else who might have knowledge of what the hell was going on and chose to share it with Spence and his team.

"This is my fault," Rick muttered.

Spence shook his head. He hated how Rick took everything on his shoulders as if he were responsible for every bad thing that happened in their orbit. "How do you figure?"

"I'm the one who convinced him to help us, and now he's dead."

"It could have nothing to do with the case."

Rick rolled his eyes. "Yeah, and I'm a chimpanzee in a man's skin suit."

"Where do you come up with that shit?" Gunner chuckled.

"It's my superpower."

"How about you wait in the SUV while we talk with the detective?" Spence suggested as he pulled out the keys and handed them to Rick. "We shouldn't be too long. Lock the doors."

"Okay," Rick mumbled as he took the keys and glanced toward the Dumpster. "Clearly, this is what you guys do." Rick turned, and Spence watched until he was safely inside the SUV.

"Okay. Let's get down to business."

\*\*\*

*Rick*

Rick sat silently in the passenger seat of the SUV and tried hard not to berate himself. It'd taken him years to accept what Arthur had told him repeatedly: *You're not to blame for being a child who was taken advantage of by a predator.*

Yet, he couldn't help feeling, if he hadn't been so zeroed in on finding Ellen, he might've considered he was putting Donald in danger. Rick groaned and buried his face in his hands. Even knowing he couldn't be held responsible for what someone else had done to Donald, it didn't alleviate the guilt. And it made what was going on with this case that much more ominous.

A beep from his cell had him looking up. He opened the screen and noticed he had one voice mail message and one new email. He tapped on the message, and moments later, Donald's voice was coming through loud and clear.

*"Hey, Rick, it's Donald. I've found some information on your NOAH Project I think you'll find interesting. I'll email you a copy in the meantime until we can speak again. You were right. There's more going on here than a missing person. Talk soon."*

Rick sucked in a deep breath and let it out slowly before doing it again. After repeating that five times, he felt steady enough to open his email. He hovered his index finger over the email and was about to open it when someone tapped on his side window. When Rick turned around, he found an older gentleman trying the handle on the door.

"Open up."

"I don't think so, buddy," Rick said as he slid away from the passenger door.

"We're friends of Donald's."

"We?" Rick asked before looking around the parking lot and finding another older man standing off to the right staring at the team. "What do you want?"

"To talk," he said as he tried the door handle again.

"Who are you?"

He didn't answer. It was time to call in the cavalry. Rick reached over and laid on the SUV's horn. When he looked back at the door, the guy was gone, and so was his friend.

The team came running at full speed. When they were within a few feet, he unlocked the doors. Spence dove into the driver's seat while Fletch and Gunner took up positions around the vehicle.

"What's wrong?"

Rick hadn't realized he was shaking until Spence took hold of his hand. "There were two older men, and one was trying to get in while the other stood off to the side watching you guys."

"Could they be the men Donald mentioned talking with Tom?"

"I don't know, but anything's possible. When I restarted my phone—you remember I had to recharge it—there was a voice message from Donald and an email."

"What'd he say?"

"That he found information on the NOAH Project and wanted to talk to me."

Rick pressed the email icon and opened Donald's email. He skimmed it and felt dread blanketing his body.

"I... I hope I'm reading this wrong" Rick felt his stomach rolling.

"Why? What does it say?"

"If this is real, my life was a fairy tale by comparison." He handed his phone over to Spence, who skimmed through the six-page attachment.

When he was done, he rolled down his window and said, "Hop in. We're leaving."

Gunner and Fletch opened the back doors and got in without questioning why. Spencer took off before the doors were even closed. Rick's hands began shaking again, and Spence reached over to hold them with his strong right hand.

"Anyone want to tell us what's going on?" Gunner asked.

"I got a visit from two men who I think were the guys who talked to Tom. They tried to get me out of the vehicle, so I honked the horn for help."

"Shit. You good?" Fletch asked.

"Freaked out, but yeah, I'm good."

"Rick received a voice mail from Donald sometime last night, and he send an email with information on the NOAH Project."

"Damn," Gunner huffed.

"Dude was thorough. What's the NOAH Project?" Fletch asked. "Or do I want to know?"

"I don't even want to know," Spence said. "They were experimenting on fertility. I'll forward the email to you."

"Like for diseases and stuff?" Fletch asked.

"More like creating the perfect human."

Gunner asked, "Does it say who was funding the project?"

"Yeah. The U.S. Navy."

\*\*\*

*Spence*

Spence stared at his screen in disgusted shock at what a man named Dr. Frauste had been doing decades ago before their funding was terminated. Frauste was dishonorably discharged from the Navy along with one other person whose name had been redacted. Knowing this much led to a series of questions for which Spence knew they'd never get answers: Where did the money come from? Was this a sanctioned project or a rogue experiment? Who else was involved? Spence knew how the Navy worked. No way a small band of outlying scientists could carry on a project without the say-so of a few someones in the chain of command.

The last known record of the NOAH Project was staring back at him, and for the first time, Spence wasn't sure what they should do. He'd called Brick, who decided he and Shaw would come to help them with this case. They'd be arriving that evening.

"This is fucked up," Gunner stated from the kitchen table as he read through what Donald had sent them.

"The Navy greenlit this project?" Rick asked.

"Maybe not. It's possible Dr. Frauste might have been a lone wolf. The Navy may have authorized a completely different project, and if the commanding officer kept sending in falsified reports, the top brass wouldn't know unless someone took an interest and looked into things. There are thousands of projects on the go at any one time," Spence explained.

"Does that mean whoever was in charge was in cahoots with the doctor?" Rick asked.

"Cahoots? We've gotta get you a better vocabulary, man." Fletch laughed.

"Affiliated, allied, in accord, banded together, hooked up, yada yada, but cahoots has a better ring," Rick explained.

Fletch laughed louder. "You're one of a kind, bro."

"Now you're getting it," Rick said with a grin.

Spence continued to stare at the numbers associated with the test subjects. It was an alphanumeric code representing the ongoing experiments, but deciphering its meaning required more information than he had.

"There's a list of numbers on the second page. What do you make of them?" Spence asked.

"Could it be the subjects' birthdates?" Fletch offered.

"Do you think the numbers indicate something like their Social Security numbers?" Rick asked.

Spence looked down at the numbers. "It couldn't be that easy. I can't believe they'd be so obvious."

He brought up a second screen went to work and couldn't believe what he found. Hubris, he thought. They were so sure no one would discover what they were really doing, they were blatant. By the time he was done with his first foray, he had six names, and June Rask and Elise Hammon were among the six.

"Luckily, it was their SSN. Unfortunately, I found Ellen's mother and grandmother were among the six women."

"Commander Rask has something to do with this," Rick said. "He can't deny it now."

Gunner said, "There are red checkmarks at the end of their names. Some have one while others had two or three."

"Births maybe, considering they were trying to make a smarter, stronger person," Gunner said. "Crazy-ass fucks. This shit's totally insane."

"No argument here," Spence agreed. "Considering there were two red checkmarks beside Elise's name, she must have, in fact, had two children."

"Like Ellen's map indicated," Rick said.

"Exactly."

"Who were the other four women?" Gunner asked.

"Janet Reese, a former Navy diver. Amanda Hart, a former Navy nurse." Spence began naming off the list.

"I'm sensing a theme here," Rick grumbled.

"Yeah, and the last two are the same," he said as he dove deeper into the four women until he hit a roadblock. "Shit. They're dead."

"Say what?" Rick gasped.

"The other four women involved in this project have died within the last year," Spence stated.

"And June, Elise's mother," Gunner added.

"We need to find Mrs. Hammon," Rick said, fear evident in his cracked voice.

Spence whipped out his phone and dialed Elise's cell, but it went straight to voice mail. "She's not picking up."

"Neither is Tom," Gunner said while waving his phone in the air.

"Seems there's a conspiracy to wipe out everyone involved in NOAH," Rick said.

"The evidence is sure leading that way," Spence agreed.

"What about Ellen?" Fletch asked.

"She could be the victim of this project. The child whose genes were screwed with, and she doesn't know what was done to her. If they're trying to clean up their mess, they'd have to get rid of her. She's living evidence of what they did."

"Hey. Take a look at the death certificates, The same coroner signed off on all four deaths," Rick pointed out.

"That's impossible. The women lived in different cities far apart," Spence said as he flipped through the screens.

"Seems like we've opened Pandora's box, and the evil is snaking out," Fletch muttered.

Rick followed with, "With each step we take, this case gets sketchier."

"Okay. Let's summarize what we have so far. Our possible kidnapping has turned into a case where five people we know of have died due to a project named NOAH. Dr. Frauste was leading the experiments, tampering with babies' DNA long before their births until the Navy found out and shut it down. Now Ellen is still missing, and we have a shitload of questions for Commander Rask."

"Do you think Tom delivered Ellen to those men who tried to get into the SUV earlier?" Rick asked.

"With everything we know, I believe he did."

"You think Tom Hammon's involved in the project?" Gunner asked.

"I don't think he knew anything until those two men had a conversation with him and filled him in. It makes sense going for the weakest link," Spence said.

"The bastard served up Ellen on a silver platter," Fletch growled.

"Then why tell us three possible men fathered Ellen?" Rick asked.

"To throw us off or buy time."

"From these records, there was no sexual intercourse involved. Everything happened in test tubes."

"How romantic," Rick scoffed. "Why would Elise want to be involved in this?"

"Because her mother had been one of the originals," Spence stated.

"The bigger question is how the commander got involved, and how did he convince his wife and daughter to be guinea pigs?"

"That's what we need to ask him. I wonder if this could be related to the tell-all book in the works?" Spence mused.

"Well, he's not answering his cell," Gunner said. "Why is nobody answering their phones?"

*Shit.* "The book probably set everything in motion. Somebody wrote a tell-all, and we assumed it was about the Hammons. Now it's looking like it was about the NOAH Project," Spence said.

"Okay, let's go get some answers. The Hammons should be in town because there's an open investigation, and they have high profile visibility. If they both disappear, a large audience will notice and ask questions. As for Commander Rask, I have his last known address."

"We'll have to split up. I'll arrange for the rental company to drop off a second vehicle. Gunner and Fletch, you get the commander and we'll take the Hammons," Spence said as he pointed between himself and Rick. "Stay sharp and trust no one."

"Status quo," Gunner said.

"Exactly."

# CHAPTER SIXTEEN

*Rick*

As they drove through the gates of the private community the Hammons lived in, Rick had the sensation he was being watched. He looked out of the passenger window but saw no one in the area. He didn't discount his instincts. He had to be hyperaware when he was under Simon's thumb, and he was scrupulous in maintaining his new persona.

"Something doesn't feel right," he told Spence.

"Agreed," Spence said as he glanced around the area. "Eyes wide open."

They continued to drive past mansions and a golf course, but Rick couldn't shake the feeling. Then he had a thought, rolled down his window, and looked above the SUV. Sure enough, there it was.

"There's a drone above us."

"Shit."

"Could be part of the security features in this community."

"Could be, but I'm betting it's not."

When they reached the Hammons', the drone disappeared, and they found Commander Rask getting out of a truck and walking to the front door. He stopped when he saw them pulling up.

They stepped out of the SUV and walked up to Rask. "Funny finding you here."

"My daughter lives here."

"I didn't get the impression you visit much," Rick said.

"I don't. I haven't been here in while, but I have to support my daughter. She needs me."

"Did she call to tell you something was wrong?" Spence asked.

"Yeah. The cameraman from their show was murdered."

"And she's broken up about it," Rick said with a question in his tone.

"Of course, she is. She isn't a cold-hearted woman," Rask growled.

"Understood," Spence said. "After you."

Rask walked ahead of them on the path, and Rick could tell something wasn't adding up. Spence's expression confirmed Rick's supposition. When Rask reached the front door, he raised his finger to push the doorbell button, but hesitated.

"What's wrong?" Rick asked.

"Nothing," he answered while stabbing the button and growling at the snap of electricity.

"They must not've fixed that yet," Spence said. "They really should put a sign on it."

Rick didn't miss the nuances of what just happened. Rask had said he hadn't been here in several months; how did he know the doorbell would shock him if he touched it? According to what they'd been told, the doorbell had been this way for only the last couple of weeks.

The door opened, revealing Elise in her nightgown. "What's going on?"

"May we come in?" Spence asked, but didn't mean it as he shoved past Elise with Rick on his tail.

When they reached the living room, they found a young man sitting on the couch with Tom.

"What's the meaning of this?" Tom blustered.

"You wouldn't answer your phone, so we got worried," Spence explained.

"As you can see, we're fine. You can leave." Tom waved as if they were bugs flying around his head.

Elise and Rask entered the room. "Is this a party?"

"You weren't expecting your father-in-law?" Spence asked.

"It was Elise who contacted me," Rask was quick to say.

"Why would Elise call you?" Tom asked.

"Because your love child decided to visit while my child is missing," Elise yelled from across the room. "Did you honestly think this was okay?"

"Ah, Dylan, nice to finally meet you," Rick said as he walked over to shake the kid's hand.

Dylan shook his hand then asked, "Who are you?"

"We're investigating Ellen's disappearance. My name's Rick, and Spence is the big guy over there."

Another knock sounded on the door. Whoever it was wasn't touching the doorbell either.

"Right on time," Spence said. "Elise. Let in the remainder of our team." Which surprised Rick. He didn't think Spence reached the team by calling or texting. He'd have to ask him about it later.

"Fine," she huffed and turned around.

"Dylan, do you visit your father often?"

"You don't have to answer that, son," Tom was quick to advise.

"True," Spence said, and Rick wanted to wipe the smirk right off Tom's face. "However, with one call, I can have you all brought into the station for questioning. Your choice."

Rick noticed that the staff was nowhere in sight. "Where are Rita, Marie, and Joe?"

"Fired. We don't require their services any longer."

Elise returned with Gunner, Fletch, Brick, and Shaw in tow.

"Look who we ran into," Fletch said while pointing at Brick and Shaw.

"What'd we miss?" Gunner asked.

"Let's see. Rask is a liar, but we all knew that. He stated he hadn't been here in months, but hesitated to ring the bell due to the shock he knew he'd receive. A malfunction that's been occurring for only a short period of time," Rick provided.

If Brick was surprised by Rick's involvement, he didn't give it away.

"Also, this is Dylan, Tom's son," Spence stated.

"After giving everyone the option of going downtown for questioning or doing it here, we're waiting for their answer," Spence said.

"My name's Brick, and I lead this team. Tell us what you know about Ellen's disappearance, or I'll have you sitting in a jail cell until you do."

"To be fair and give the public its right to know, we'll share where you're incarcerated," Fletch stated.

Elise threw up her arms and huffed, "This keeps getting better and better. I told you not to fuck with those people, Tom."

"Are you referring to the two older men you were seen in the company of a couple of weeks back?" Spence asked.

"How did you know that?" Tom growled as he stood.

"It's our job to know," Gunner said. "Sit your ass down." And he did.

Elise grabbed a drink off the counter and went to sit in a recliner in the corner. Tom had lost his cool and was vibrating. "Stop talking, you old lush."

"Now, now. Save the domestic for when we don't have to witness it. We have some questions for you. Would you prefer to answer them alone?"

"Why bother, they both know," Tom replied waving his hand between Rask and Elise. He returned to the sofa to sit beside Dylan.

Rick heard a bottle pop its cork and looked over to Elise, filling her glass with champagne. Just goes to show you: she was always so well put together when she was out in public.

"First off, none of this was my idea," Tom said. "I've been having to toe the line for far too long, and it's time I have my say."

"Okay. Let's start with where is Ellen?" Rick asked.

"I don't know. I did everything they ordered me to do, and they promised to leave my son alone."

"What about Ellen?" Rick asked. "Was she protected?"

"No, because she was a product of those experiments."

"Of course, she wasn't protected. You didn't give a shit about her anyway," Rick huffed. "Did you order your driver to change the oil in all household vehicles knowing Ellen needed a ride to school?"

"Yes. They contacted me and told me to do it."

"Give me your phone," Spence ordered while holding his hand out.

"No," Tom said.

"Give him your phone, or I'll kick you so hard in the balls Dylan's grandchildren will feel it," Rick warned as he inched closer. "Trust me. I'm hoping you don't so I can kick your balls and take the phone anyway." Rick enjoyed the fear that shot across Tom's face. This piece of shit of a human being delivered an innocent girl to murderers.

"Here, take it," Tom said while covering his jean-covered crotch for protection. It wouldn't help.

Spence took the phone, dropped it into his jacket pocket, and continued with his questioning. "These two men, who were they and what did they say?'

"They didn't give me their names, but they said they worked for those interested in keeping what happened a secret."

"What did they mean, 'what happened'? What did they want to hide?"

Tom was quiet for a moment, and with a nod of his head, he answered, "My book."

"You're the one writing the tell-all." Rick almost fell over. He hadn't seen that coming.

"The one and same," Tom admitted.

"Don't go acting all noble. You wanted the money and fame. This had nothing to do with bringing the truth forward," Elise slurred.

"Where's the book?" Spence asked.

"I don't know. I had it saved on my laptop, and now it's gone along with Ellen."

"Ellen took it?" Rick asked.

"That's the only logical explanation," Tom sniveled. God, Rick had to hold back from kicking the loathsome man in the balls.

Rick looked at Spence knowing he was about to drop the bomb. "The truth about the NOAH Project?" That got everyone's attention. "Yes, we know."

"You knew how Ellen was conceived," Rick stated.

"Yeah, but I had no choice but to go along with it."

"That's why you had an affair?"

"So I could produce a strong, healthy son, and I proved that."

"Commander Rask, how were you recruited into this project?" Brick asked.

Rask let out a deep breath. "I was assigned to the project early in my career."

"Is that how June became involved?" Shaw asked.

"Yes."

"Is Elise your biological child?" Rick asked. He wouldn't be surprised if he weren't.

"Yes. They used my sperm and June's eggs."

"Then genetically screwed with it. You're lucky she didn't come out with two heads," Rick grumbled.

"They'd promised they weren't changing who the child was, only getting rid of traits we didn't want her to have while adding a few stronger capabilities to give her an edge," Rask explained.

"Like what?" Rick challenged.

"There's diabetes in the family, and we wanted to make sure she never had it. Cancer as well," Rask continued.

"But you didn't stop there, did you?" Rick could feel his anger rising.

"Hell no," Elise shouted from the other side of the room. "I can run a marathon and never get winded. Hear conversations clearly from far away. No matter how much I eat, I'm always toned, and I never use a gym. I'm a stronger, faster, smarter lab rat."

"So, you're a success story." Rick sneered

"Not quite," Commander Rask said as he sat in a nearby chair. "At first, she had horrible migraines, and her muscle growth had her towering over the other children."

"Don't forget about this, dear father," Elise stood, took off her nightgown without a hint of modesty, and turned around.

Rick wasn't sure what he was looking at. It was about baseball size, but it wasn't protruding far out of her back, so her clothes concealed it. Even though Elise was a brunette, blonde, curly hair covered it. On closer inspection, Rick could make out a part that looked conspicuously like an ear.

"This is my twin. I like to call her Isabella." Elise preened. "Isn't she beautiful?" she asked as she reached around and ran her fingers through the blonde curls.

Rick was way past freaked out, but he held it together. Who in their right mind did this?

"Looks like they were fucking around with those petri dishes and test tubes more than you knew," Spence concluded.

Rask hung his head but didn't answer.

"Okay, let me get this straight. Elise was the product of an experiment, and then you go and do the same thing with your own child? Why?" Spence asked.

"Isabella surfaced about a decade ago. Before that, I was perfect. Beautiful, healthy, and smart. I wanted my daughter to be perfect, and I couldn't leave it to chance with Tom."

"Is 'Isabella' the only side effect you have?"

"I wish. My body cramps up, and then my muscles freeze in position. It feels like they never stop growing. I'm two inches taller from last year, and if it doesn't stop, I will be famous for something else entirely." Elise lowered the waist of her underwear to show multiple deep, jagged stretch marks on her hip. "My skin has a hard time keeping up. I'm waiting for the day it rips."

"Did these symptoms start around the same time as 'Isabella' formed?" Shaw asked.

"Yes. As I'm aging, issues continue to crop up."

Rask kept his head buried in his hands. Rick assumed he was too ashamed to look anyone in the eye.

Now came the big question. Rick looked over at Spence, waiting for the next bomb to drop.

"What happened to your second child?"

Elise's eyes filled with tears, and she moved closer to Tom, who treated her with disdain and disgust instead of offering warmth and care.

"They told me he didn't survive," Elise said through sobs.

"Who? Dr. Frauste's people?"

"And my father. I never had the chance to say good-bye," Elise whimpered like a wounded animal. "He would've been my first child. It took another five years to get pregnant with Ellen."

"What happened with that baby, Rask?" Brick asked, not bothering to hide his fury.

Rask sucked in a deep breath and stood. "He's—"

Rick heard the slight ping of glass breaking before a red spot appeared on Rask's chest. His mind couldn't comprehend what was happening, and then the commander collapsed onto the floor."

"Get down," Rick heard someone yell, and before Rick knew it, he was flat on his stomach with a body covering him

That's when the noises began making sense. Someone was firing at them through the wall of windows. He heard the team returning fire. It felt like the exchange went on for several minutes, but it was probably no more than thirty seconds.

"Are you hurt?" Spence asked from above him. When he finally managed to sit, the big guy searched through his clothing for any possible wounds.

"No. I'm okay."

Spence stopped his search and pulled Rick into his arms. "Thank god."

"What about you? Are you injured?" Rick began looking all around Spence's body, but he didn't see any red marks.

"No. But our leads are being picked off," he said while pointing at Rask, who was lying in a pool of blood on the floor.

Rick hadn't liked the man but felt pity for the guy. The man had lived a lie for so long it had to've been eating away at him until he was a shell of his former self. A very sad existence for sure.

"Call an ambulance," Brick yelled, and Rick looked over as Spence took out his phone to find their team leader performing CPR on Elise while Tom and Dylan watched from the back of the couch.

*Shit.*

Whatever information the father and daughter had went to the grave, leaving the team no closer to finding Ellen.

# CHAPTER SEVENTEEN

*Spence*

They spent the remainder of the night with the local LEOs answering questions about what happened. Whoever shot at them got away using a waiting boat. No one got a good look at the shooters. They couldn't be sure it was the same men from before.

It was well past three in the morning before they got back to the rental.

"Everyone hit the sack. We'll need fresh eyes in the morning," Brick ordered, and no one argued. Spence was more than ready for some shut-eye.

"Hey, boss. You and Shaw can bunk in my room if you want. I won't be sleeping there."

"Where will you be sleeping?" Brick asked.

Spence wrapped his arm around Rick, answering the question without saying a word.

"Oh. Okay. Everyone get as much rest as possible because tomorrow will be a long one."

Spence pulled Rick into his arms and asked, "Do you need to get anything from the kitchen before bed?"

"No. I have what I need right beside me."

Spence couldn't stop his goofy smile. No one he'd ever dated bothered to say these types of things. Spence didn't know what he was missing out on until Rick.

Spence took hold of Rick's hand and led them upstairs to his room. Once he had him inside, he raced over to his old room, grabbed his belongings before bringing them into what was now officially their room, and dumped them on a chair.

Rick watched him with a serene smile on his face. When he began to remove his clothing, Spence followed suit. As each layer was removed, the harder his cock became until he was completely naked, sporting a substantial hard-on.

"We'll sleep, that's all," Spence said. He waved at his dick. "This will go down."

Rick lowered his jeans, revealing the most delicious hard-on, and Spence wanted to taste it, but he didn't move.

"I'm afraid mine won't go down, so we'll have to deal with it before getting any sleep."

Spence was on him in seconds, kneeling and sucking Rick's cock to the back of his throat. Rick moaned deep, and Spence could feel his lover's legs begin to buckle. He gathered him into his arms and laid him across the bed without missing a beat.

He slid his hands up Rick's inner thigh on his way to reclaim his prize when Rick freaked. He grabbed Spence's hands and relocated them onto his outer thighs. Spence knew why an instant later when he noticed the scars on the inside of his thighs and remembered Rick telling him about his cutting.

Spence's heart broke, and he saw one of the lines was new. "When did you do this?"

"The night Simon contacted me," Rick answered before turning his head.

Spence reached up and touched Rick's chin. "Don't do that. You've had to live through hell, and this was how you coped. From now on, when you feel like you want to cut, come to me instead. I'll talk you down."

"They're ugly," Rick said, his eyes filling with tears. "I don't want you to look at them. Can we turn out the lights?"

"I'll do you one better." Spence lowered his head and kissed Rick's scars one by one. There were groupings of scars where he took his time, making sure he didn't miss one. "The only thing I see here is the man I'm falling in love with."

Rick sat up. "Love?"

"Yep, love." There was no way in hell he was backing down now. "I'm in love with you."

"Are you sure?" Rick asked, looking every bit the young teenager left out on the streets.

"With every fiber of my being, I know I love you and never want to be away from you."

Rick sat up and dove into Spence's arms. "You mean it?"

"Every word."

Spence didn't bother waiting for Rick to say he loved him. He knew Rick would tell him when he was ready.

"Can we pick up where we left off?" Rick asked with those puppy dog eyes pleading.

"You bet your gorgeous ass we are."

Spence lowered Rick down onto the mattress and ran his hands up Rick's inner thighs. This time, there was no stopping as he lowered his lips to kiss, lick, and explore the body below him.

Rick's moans grew louder, and soon he was clutching the sheets underneath him. Nothing had ever been this sexy as seeing Rick in the throes of passion. His eyes were closed, and his tongue was peeking out, licking his lips and making Spence's balls pull up tight. The sensation backed off with one sure tug on his sac, buying him more time to pleasure his lover.

No way he would come too soon, no matter how excited he was. But those low moans were driving him crazy. Spence sucked Rick's cock as his hips thrust up. He grabbed onto Rick's butt cheeks and held him in place while he took his time bringing every ounce of pleasure out of him.

Rick's moans were getting louder as Spence increased his speed and pressure, bringing him closer to the edge, and then Spence sank his index finger inside Rick, and fireworks went off. Rick's back bowed off the bed as white streaks of his release painted his abs. Spence held him close until his body relaxed onto the mattress.

"Ready for round two?" Spence asked as he flipped Rick onto his stomach.

"Hell yeah," Rick muttered, his voice deep and sexy.

"I was hoping you'd say that." Spence chuckled before jumping off the bed to retrieve his bag. He grabbed the lube and condoms and climbed onto the bed. "Ready?" He wanted to make sure Rick was fully on board.

"If you don't stick that thick beast inside me soon, we'll be having problems," Rick growled.

Squeezing lube onto his finger, Spence went to work loosening Rick's hole so Spence wouldn't hurt him when he slid his cock inside. Once he could get two of his fingers in Rick's tight channel, he searched for his prize, and by Rick's sudden shouts, he'd found the tiny gland that would set his lover's world on fire.

"That's it. Oh yes, please," Rick begged for more, and Spence slid a third finger in and began rubbing his prostate with abandon.

Rick's cries and whimpers were like music to Spence's ears, and all he wanted was more. Spence pulled back his fingers, grabbed a condom, rolled it down his throbbing cock, and lined himself up with Rick's hole.

"God, I've been dreaming about doing this for so long," Spence said as he slid forward, not stopping until he bottomed out.

Spence froze, allowing Rick to grow accustomed to his size and the stretch, but the longer he waited, the closer he came to his own orgasm. He almost cried out when Rick bucked his hips, and he pulled out halfway before slamming back in.

"Yesss." Rick's voice was ragged. "Don't stop."

"Oh no. We're just getting started."

Spence was a man of his word. Over the next hour, he showed Rick how much he meant to him. There wasn't a part of his body Spence hadn't touched, and he still wanted more. His body and soul felt renewed and content for the first time ever by having this amazing man as his lover.

He laid his chest onto Rick's back, pressing their skin together as those telltale tingles started at the base of his spine. He was going to come. Quickly he flipped Rick over and reentered him.

"I want to see your face when we come," he said as he wrapped his hand around Rick's cock and began pumping in pace with his hips.

They came in a melody of cries and moans while staring at each other. This was the man he belonged with, and Spence would do anything to protect that.

After a short recovery, Spence went to the bathroom and cleaned up before bringing a warm washcloth and towel for Rick, who was snoring by now. He wiped his lover clean and dried him off before joining him in bed.

Once he had Rick securely in his arms, Spence rested. Who knew what was coming for them tomorrow? He thought about Commander Rask and felt no joy at his death, no matter how much the asshole had put him through.

What a waste. All those people involved in the NOAH Project, which was shut down over a decade ago, turning up dead now. Lives were destroyed to protect the men who thought they had the right to build a better human.

People had been playing god. It wasn't the first time in history others had tried to do that through wars and genocides. He'd seen it play out across the globe in one form or another throughout his military career.

When would people learn?

# CHAPTER EIGHTEEN

*Rick*

Rick sat back watching the team categorize, rearrange, dissect, and put back together everything they'd learned. Through the process they put forth suggestions and bounced ideas off each other. They worked well together, which shouldn't've been a surprise considering they'd been doing it for so many years.

"Who do we have left alive and on the list?" Brick asked.

"Tom, Dylan, and those two men that keep popping up. Dr. Frauste, if he's still alive," Spence answered.

"What about the second person dishonorably discharged along with Frauste?" Gunner asked.

"It's not as if we can quiz Rask on the project's personnel," Fletch huffed. "It feels like we're going around in circles.

"I've called in a few favors," Spence said. "We'll see what I get back."

Rick wanted to mention something, but he wasn't sure about the new dynamic with Brick and Shaw here. He wondered if they considered him part of the team and if they wanted his input.

"Can you think of anything, Rick?" Spence asked.

"Oh, um, yes. I wasn't sure if I should still help."

"Help? We can use all the help we can get. Spence has told me you've been indispensable on this case," Brick stated.

"He did?" Rick looked over at Spence for confirmation.

"Damn straight."

It's one thing to hope you're contributing, it's another hearing Spence thought so highly of Rick's assistance Spence took the time to mention it to Brick.

"Okay then. I'd like to find this nanny, Rosaline," Rick said.

"Why? Do you think she's involved?"

"Not involved in the drama, but trust me when I tell you, if I had somewhere safe to go when I was put out on the street, I would've taken it. If Rosaline isn't harboring Ellen, I bet she knows where the girl is hiding."

"Do you still believe Ellen ran away?" Shaw asked.

"It's possible, but for a different reason than hating her family. I think Ellen found out about Tom's book deal and searched for the manuscript. If she found it, she was in for the shock of her life," Rick explained. "She was working it out on the board covering the back of her dresser. And that piece of paper we found ripped from the thumbtack might've gone with her."

"Maybe she got spooked by her grandmother's death," Spence said.

"Has anyone seen this manuscript?" Brick asked.

"No," Gunner and Fletch said at the same time.

"They found nothing on his computer, at the publishers, or in his office at the TV station," Spence stated.

"Where could it be?" Brick asked.

"I think it's with Ellen," Rick said.

"Explain?" Brick instructed.

"Well, when we questioned everyone, we learned it wasn't typical for Ellen to have to walk to the bus stop. We now know changing the motor oil was a ruse concocted by the old guys. Once she'd been informed she'd be walking to the bus stop, she returned to her room, then took her backpack and left. She could've sensed something was off and decided it was time to run and took a thumb drive with the manuscript on it. She could've been the one who left the scuff on the wall when she moved the dresser and tore the paper from the tack."

The room was silent, and Rick wondered if he'd gone out on a ledge. Spence stood next to him and gave him a shoulder squeeze.

"I love the way your mind works," Spence said.

"Run with it," Brick ordered. "You and Spence follow up on that lead while the rest of us go hunting."

"Hunting?" Rick asked.

"There are two men who have a great deal to answer for, and we'll start by turning them into the prey," Brick said, followed by a few of the team members' agreement.

Rick had to admit he liked the sound of that.

It was time to teach those assholes a lesson.

\*\*\*

*Spence*

Spence had done some digging into Rosaline Rehez and hadn't found much. He started with the addresses Marie had given them, and the first two didn't pan out. The second one yielded fifteen of her relatives who lived in the immediate area, but no Rosaline. She was a widow with no children of her own and could be anywhere.

Next stop, they were heading for Rosaline's last known address, and hoped they would find some answers.

"How are we going to approach this?" Rick asked.

"What do you mean?"

"Good guy, bad guy routine. I've always seen myself as an aloof detective."

Spence looked over at Rick, who was styling his hair in the mirror on the sun visor. "Aloof detective?" He couldn't help but smile.

"You know, all serious, smokes a pipe, has a bit of a drinking problem, tattoos, and a toothpick sticking out of the corner of his mouth. Maybe I should get a fedora."

Spence was amused. This was the Rick he'd fallen for. The outspoken, quirky man who drove him nuts.

"I think you'd look good in a hat," Spence stated.

Rick turned to look at him with pure happiness radiating from his face. "Thank you for *getting* me."

"I've got your back," Spence said without hesitation.

They drove for another fifteen minutes past larger houses with manicured lawns, through middle-class condos until they came to an average subdivision where the houses all looked the same. Rosaline's house was in there somewhere, and as they drove through the maze of streets, it was obvious they were outsiders. People stared at them and took pictures of their vehicle as they passed by.

"I get the impression they don't want company," Rick said while he looked side to side.

Spence had to admit the place was giving off serious "get the hell out" vibes, but they weren't leaving until they spoke with Rosaline. "It's up on the right."

Rick looked over. "Right. One oh two," he said while pointing at the house with the green door.

Spence pulled over and parked on the street in front of the house. It'd be easier to take off fast if needed instead of having to back out of the driveway.

"The green door seems welcoming," Rick suggested.

"Sure, we can go with that. Let's check it out."

They both got out of the SUV and walked side by side to the door. The neighbor to the right came out of his garage and plunked down a lawn chair as if waiting for the festivities to begin.

"Maybe you should go back to the vehicle. I'm not sure what to expect when that door opens."

"I'm not leaving your side. Get over it."

"I'm trying to protect you."

"I know, but I'm not leaving."

"Are you always going to be this difficult?"

"You knew the package before you signed on." Rick laughed and reached for the doorbell.

Before he had the chance to ring it, the door opened, revealing a man in his twenties. "Can I help you?"

"We're here to talk with Rosaline Rehez," Spence said.

"I don't know who you're talking about. Please leave." Well, that was a lie. The guy didn't even try that hard.

"We aren't the police," Rick stated. "We're trying to find a missing girl before the bad guys do."

"And who's to say you aren't the bad guys?"

"Good point," Rick said, looking at Spence for some assistance.

"We received this address from the staff she used to work with at the Hammons' residence. They understood we're trying to protect Ellen, not harm her," Spence said. "There's a lot of players out there searching for Ellen. I wouldn't expect those who wish her harm to walk up to the house where her nanny lives in broad daylight. Last night's shooting from a distance through windows is more their style."

"Shooting?"

"Yeah. Two people were killed at the Hammons' residence."

"We were in the crossfire." Rick shivered.

"Who was killed?"

"Elise Hammon and her father."

"Wait here," the unnamed man said as he retreated inside the house.

Rick looked at Spence, checking in that they were all right. Spence smiled and nodded, unsure of what to say, but inching his body closer to Rick's in case anything went south, and he needed to protect him.

A few moments later, the door reopened, but instead of the man from before, an older woman stood staring at them.

"I understand you are looking for me," she said.

"Rosaline?"

"Yes."

"My name's Spence, and this is Rick. We're part of L. H. Investigations, and we were called in by the police chief to aid in finding a missing girl, Ellen Hammon."

Rosaline looked them over shrewdly.

"I understand you have no reason to trust us," Rick said. "But I sense you're a good person, and from what we've been told, Ellen loves you like a mother. If that's true, you need to protect her. Please ensure Ellen remains in hiding until we can get to the root of this mess. There are former government personnel involved, and we aren't sure if they've gone rogue in a cover-up attempt. In any case, people are dying. If you can hide her even deeper, please do, and keep her safe."

"Are you trying to tell me you're not here to drag a frightened child out?"

Spence took over. "No dragging, I assure you. We'd like to know if she's safe and make sure she stays hidden. Here is my card. Call me anytime for any reason and our team will come help protect you and her. If you need money to help care for her and hide her, I can send whatever you need to your account."

They both walked away from the door. Spence knew no one was getting inside that house today, but if they'd convinced Rosaline to hide Ellen even more, he was good with that for now. The girl wasn't safe out in the open.

They got back into the SUV and drove away.

"We'll be back here," Rick said.

"Most definitely."

# CHAPTER NINETEEN
*Rick*

The winds blew and bent the trees around their rental house, and the windows shook with the force. The weather reflected Rick's turmoil. It'd been two days since they'd spoken to Rosaline, and they still hadn't heard anything from her. He hoped she took their warning to heart because he was positive the former nanny knew where Ellen was.

Brick and Gunner were at police headquarters while Shaw and Fletch chased down new leads. Rick sat wondering what the next logical move would be. The NOAH papers confirmed that all women involved in the project were dead, leaving only Ellen alive. They were running out of people who could direct them to the project personnel who were still alive, and most likely responsible for all the deaths and destruction.

Tom and his son, Dylan, were being kept at a safe house in case they were next on the killers' list. Spence had been tracing Dr. Frauste's movements from the moment he was discharged from the Navy. So far, he'd tracked him across Europe and to Asia. It was hard going because there wasn't a lot of record-keeping available in certain areas.

There was that one individual who was kicked out along with Frauste when it was discovered that they were trying to engineer a better human. Who that person could be was still a question mark. Rick had studied the information Donald had sent him and the evidence they found in Ellen's bedroom repeatedly without any luck.

The last few letters of two words left on the ripped piece of paper they found under Ellen's desk had produced nothing, and there was still the question of an unknown sibling reported deceased at birth whom no one knew about. For all they knew, there could be a twenty-two-year-old superhuman out there somewhere.

Rick looked at the picture of the piece of paper again. It had two words, one over the other. Only the top three letters and the bottom one letter remained. T, H, Y, and K. He tried associating them with names, but nothing made sense. They were missing something, but he couldn't puzzle it out for the life of him.

"Hey, how's it going?" Spence asked as he joined Rick at the table.

"Nowhere. I've got nothing." Rick was frustrated that they'd hit a dead end.

"Don't worry. Something will turn up."

"Before or after someone else dies?" Rick growled. "Sorry, you don't deserve that."

"It's okay. We're a team and part of a bigger team. No matter what, we support each other, and never give up."

"I don't see how in this case. Most everyone involved is dead, except Tom, who started it all with his tell-all."

"Doesn't seem right, somehow."

"I know what you mean," Spence agreed. "Listen, I have some news for you about Simon."

Rick chest tightened. "And?"

"We've tracked him to the west side of Chicago."

"So, we're getting closer, right?"

"Yeah. We should have an exact location soon. Especially since we've captured Spike."

Rick's chest loosened slightly. "You found Spike? Where?"

Spence hesitated.

"Spike was in Marshall, wasn't he?"

"Yeah. Elias arrested him before he got anywhere near the lake house."

He nodded his relief. "Has he given you any information on Simon?"

"They're still questioning him. Don't worry, we'll find the bastard."

Rick didn't respond. He wouldn't hope. He couldn't. Not until Simon was behind bars. Then, and only then, could Rick get on with his life.

"Hey, guys, what's up?" Brick asked as he and Gunner walked through the front door.

"Nothing new." Rick wasn't going to bring up what he was sure they already knew.

"Well, Commander Rask's current wife has left town with the commander's body. He'll be laid to rest back home," Gunner said.

"Yeah, how did Dorothy take it?" Spence asked, and a spark went off in Rick's head.

He remembered something. What *was* it? His brain was telling him the answer was right in front of him, but all he saw were pieces of paper full of notes.

The others continued with their conversation, but Rick was on to something. He rifled through the pages on the table over and over, knowing the answer was there, somewhere.

"Rick, are you okay?" Spence asked.

"No. I remembered something or heard something important, but I can't find it," he said in a rush.

"Okay, we talked about leads. Rask's burial, um..." Gunner said.

"Was it the burial?"

"It has to be, but what?" Rick asked, searching but not finding the thread. "But something clicked then, and I don't know why."

Rick looked through the pages and pictures until he came to the one he finally realized he needed. "This one right here." Rick laid the scrap of paper found under the dresser out for them all to see.

"What is it?" Gunner asked.

"This THY and the second word K was handwritten as if Ellen herself figured it out. Could it stand for Dorothy Rask?"

The other three looked at the paper and then back to each other. Rick knew he was on to something.

"What if Ellen figured out Grandpa's new wifey was actually on the original team from the beginning? I noticed all the personnel at the beginning of this project were under thirty. They'd be roughly the same age now, in their late sixties. What better way to keep an eye on the test subjects, and the commander would have to go along with it because he was as dirty as her and Frauste," Brick said while working it out. "Spence, I want to know everything about who this Dorothy Rask really is. Gunner, contact the police chief, fill him in, and ask for her to be brought in for questioning."

Spence squeezed Rick's arms. "See, I told you something would pop up. This time your amazingly organized mind zeroed in on what we couldn't see. Come with me, and we'll dig up dirt on the latest Mrs. Rask."

Rick smiled wide. When Spence looked at him as if he were some gift, Rick's heart soared. He followed Spence out into the living room, where he brought his beast of a computer to life. Rick felt good knowing he'd helped the team.

While Spence worked on his laptop, Rick researched topics Spence found, working on them on his much slower laptop, but he was helping, and that's all that mattered. The rest of the team were in and out as they searched, letting them know that Dorothy Rask had disappeared from her hotel room.

"She must've known we were getting close," Spence concluded. "She couldn't've gotten far."

The other team members went to chase a few leads on Dorothy while Rick and Spence remained at the rental house. Rick felt a lot better now that they had this new lead. It was driving him crazy to sit back and wait for something to happen.

"Do you think Commander Rask had anything to do with the killings?" Rick asked.

"You know it struck me when he made that comment when he was leaving. *If your team's half as good as they say you guys are, you'll find Ellen before irreparable damage is done. I'm counting on that."*

"Maybe he knew he had no power to stop what was coming and he was being honest that he hoped we found Ellen before she was hurt."

"One hell of a missing person case." Rick sighed.

"No one expected the hornets' nest we've dug up. I'm surprised we haven't received a call from the higher-ups to back off."

"Unless they want this resolved as much as we do," Rick stated.

"Possibly. Better for 'outsiders' to put this to bed than an internal investigation that might leak to the press." Spence worked for a while before he said, "There's no record of Dorothy existing before the NOAH Project."

"So, she re-created herself as Rask's new wife."

"Considering he and June had been divorced for years by then, no one would be the wiser. She could slip into the role because Rask was stationed at a new facility after the project shut down and was buried." Spence went back to his search.

"Who do you think left that tidbit of information in the records for someone to find?"

"It might've been Commander Rask leaving the trail to the truth," Spence stated.

"Now we wait until Dorothy is located. Do you think those two men work for her?"

"Yeah. I suspect those men work for her. One thing that bothers me is why they named the project NOAH. If it is a biblical reference, what do an ark and two of every animal have to do with it?"

Rick thought about the word Noah. "I wonder if it could mean only the best of society survives, or are the chosen ones."

"That tracks, considering they were attempting to create a better human."

"Hell, it could be someone's last name for all we know." Rick huffed at the cruelty of the project. "That would be pretty damn narcissistic of someone."

Spence looked at him closely. "What did you say?"

"It could be somebody's name."

Spence began typing on his laptop as Rick watched screen after screen fly by at a speed only Spence could understand. His eyes flicked across screens in seconds before he tuned into another location or site, and off the screens would go searching, always searching. It was incredible to watch as Spence became part of the systems and platforms running all the checks.

"You're amazing," Rick whispered, not wanting to distract him.

Suddenly everything stopped, and the screen went blank. Spence turned to Rick and said, "You're the one who's amazing." He hit a button on his keyboard, and suddenly reams of information populated the screen, and one name kept appearing, Isabelle Noah.

"You found her?"

"No. We found her."

Before Rick could respond, Spence pulled him over and kissed him as no man had ever kissed him before, with reverence and adoration. This was what love felt like. Full of wonder and discovery, coupled with mystification on how they were fortunate enough to've found each other. And to find respect and care for every inch of the person in front of you.

"I love you, Spencer." Rick had never said those words to anyone else. Not the way he loved Spence. The only love he'd known in his life was for his father, his mentor, Arthur, and for his best friend, Roman. This was on a whole other level, one where he'd never been, and while scary on some levels, it was the adventure of a lifetime.

"I love you too. I don't want to be without you."

"Me either. I'm not going anywhere without you."

They held each other for several minutes until the computer screen beeped at them.

"It's done."

"What's done?"

"My systems have searched out every spec of information on one Dr. Isabelle Noah, and it's time for us to do some reading," Spence said with a smile.

"I'm down for some reading."

The printer came to life and began firing out paper. "You can start there, and I'll start in another direction."

"You got it," Rick said before jumping up from his chair and going over to the printer to collect the pages.

Over the next several hours, Rick and Spence sat poring over data collected worldwide. No big surprise that this woman had been quite vaunted in the study of genetics, and had been hired straight out of university in Sweden by a now-defunct organization owned by a rich Russian before she turned up in the United States as part of this project.

"How does a Swedish geneticist go from working for a large Russian company to the U.S. Navy?" Rick asked, stunned by what he was reading.

"You'd be surprised when it comes to who knows who in a small scientific community."

"This can of worms is nasty."

"Agreed."

Much later, they were compiling the information when the rest of the team arrived back from searching for Dorothy Rask.

"Any luck?" Rick asked when they walked into the kitchen.

"Not even a sighting." Gunner sighed.

"How could she disappear so quickly?" Fletch asked.

"Wish I knew," Brick replied. "I hear you two have come up with some new information."

"Yeah. Have a seat," Spence said as he handed out copies of the brief before sitting beside Rick and turning his laptop screen around so everyone could see. "We'd like to introduce you to Isabelle Noah." Her image popped onto the screen.

"She has blond curly hair. You think Elise's Isabella is based on a real person, Isabelle Noah?"

"I wouldn't be surprised about anything in this case."

"Looks like she was throwing a bit of her genetics into the mix."

"She was a highly regarded geneticist trained in Sweden and was scooped up by the Russians during the cold war. Somehow, she ended up working as a contractor for the Navy."

"Lured by money?"

"More than likely."

"She named the project after herself," Gunner huffed. "Ego much?"

"A huge one, for sure. And when the project shut down, Isabelle Noah became Dorothy Rask," Rick said, and the picture on the screen changed to what Rask's wife looked like.

"She dyed her hair brown and must wear contacts to hide her blue eyes."

"No one caught that?"

"Back then, they wanted things hushed, so they shipped Commander Rask off to a new command, and she went along as his wife."

"Wow, that's fucked up."

"So she was never far from some of her test subjects."

"Rask let this happen?"

"He didn't have a choice. I'm guessing he was told to pretend like nothing ever happened or be erased along with his family."

"Talk about coercion."

"And now, fifteen years later, we're searching for the woman who started it all."

"This is the last known picture of Dorothy Rask/Isabelle Noah."

The screen changed again, showing a woman in her sixties. Her brown hair had turned gray, but she looked as fit as the photos taken a decade ago.

Rick watched the men surrounding the kitchen table as they went over the information. Happy for his small part in hopefully catching this woman.

"Do you think she's the one who's having the people involved in the project killed?"

Spence turned the screen to another picture. This time there were North Korean military standing front and center. In the middle, a skinny man in a lab coat was scrunched between the uniforms. His grin said it all.

"This is Dr. Frauste. After being thrown out of the Navy, he offered his services to the highest bidder."

"He carried on with the experiments from North Korea?"

"Yep. And he's still there."

"Do you think he and his former partner, Isabelle Noah, are still in touch?"

"I think that she stayed behind to watch over the test subjects while he went on to create a new lab for the two of them."

"You mentioned the other women in the project had been killed. What about their children? Could there be more kids like Ellen out there?"

"I believe so. After we're done here, and Isabelle and her men are behind bars, we'll have to find them," Brick said.

The group nodded or grunted their agreement.

"Okay, let's break this down," Spence said. "Isabelle Noah was the lead scientist on the NOAH Project until it was shut down. She stays behind while her partner starts a new life for them where the government would condone this sort of thing. Tom Hammon decided to write a tell-all book about the project, and people began dying." Spence tilted his head. "Is it possible the Navy has nothing to do with what's happening right now?"

"What do you mean?" Shaw asked.

"Wait, I get what you're saying," Rick spoke up. "What if their new bosses didn't want the information getting out?"

"And Frauste sent word to Isabelle to eliminate all trace of the NOAH Project."

"Damn. Who expected a missing girl would turn into a case of genetic manipulation and murder?"

Spence pointed at the screen. "This is the lady with the answers we need. All effort should go into finding her."

"Agreed," Brick said. "Let's go hunting."

Rick saw the team's mindset had changed from search and rescue to find, capture, and destroy. He hoped it wasn't the team who got destroyed.

# CHAPTER TWENTY
*Spence*

There'd been sightings of Isabelle Noah coming in after the local media ran with the story, and between the local police and the team, they were checking every one of them. It felt like Spence had been in the SUV all day, and with each false report, his frustration grew.

On top of that, his leads on Simon's exact location were drying up and Spence refused to allow the trail to grow cold. They knew the rat was hiding somewhere, but as of yet they hadn't been able to pinpoint his location. Spike was close to giving up the goods on his boss, but they needed more time.

He and Rick were heading back to the rental house when Spence noticed they were being followed.

"We've got a tail."

"I could so riff on that, but now's not the time." Rick chuckled. "Can you see who it is?"

"He's not close enough for me to make out his features, but it looks like one person."

Rick turned in his seat. "We wouldn't happen to have a pair of binoculars in here, would we?"

Spence reached into the glove box and handed a pair to Rick. "Here you go."

"Ah shit."

"What's wrong?" Spence asked, fearing the worse. "Is it Isabelle?"

"No, it's that PI from before," Rick huffed.

"What the hell does he want now?" Spence growled as he gunned the engine and took off. "Let's see how interested he really is."

Rick turned around and redid his seatbelt. "Isn't there too much traffic?"

"That's why we're headed to the industrial area, fewer people."

Once he cleared the remaining traffic, he floored the gas pedal. The SUV wasn't a race car, but it had some balls, and he'd use them to teach this PI a lesson.

"Call the guys to tell them what's going on and meet us at the WHISCO packaging plant out of town."

Rick got onto the phone and did as he asked while Spence took a sharp right followed by a left. The PI was still there. Their speed increased as they cleared the last traffic light, and the PI was still behind them.

"He has to know we know he's following us," Rick said. "Why doesn't he stop?"

"My guess is he wants to talk but didn't dare come around the house again after his last attempt."

"Then why don't we stop and talk to him?"

"I intend to, but on my terms, not his," Spence said with a grin.

They continued along the Quarter Line until the packaging plant came into view. The backlot was empty, and he headed straight for it. When he felt they were far enough away from people, he said, "Hold on." And slammed on the brakes.

The tires squealed and smoked, but he held on to control, spinning the SUV around until they were facing the oncoming car. The PI slammed on the brakes and slid to a stop roughly ten yards away.

Before Spence could unhook his seatbelt, other vehicles pulled up behind and beside the PI's car. The team had been waiting for them and now had the PI's car surrounded.

"This looks like a nice place for a chat." Rick laughed as he pried his hand away from the *holy fuck* handles.

The PI shut off his car and got out with his hands out to his sides. "First smart thing this asshole has done," Spence muttered. "Let's go see what Mr. Conor O'Brian wants to talk about," he said as he reached for the door handle.

He waited for Rick to join him at the front of their vehicle before walking over to the PI. Brick, Gunner, Shaw, and Fletch stood by their vehicles, watching and waiting on full alert.

As they neared, the PI began lowering his arms.

"I didn't say you could lower your arms," Spence was quick to tell him. Who knew what the dude was up to? He could be working for Isabelle.

"Why are you following us?"

It was good to see the man not so cocky. "I wanted to talk."

"I thought we were all talked out, you POS. What've you got to say? That you're the scum of the earth who was trying to take a toddler away from his family?" Rick snapped. Clearly, his adrenaline was still pumping.

"No. I know I screwed up on that one," Conor said. "But this has to do with other people watching you."

That got everyone's attention, and the rest of the team joined them. "What do you mean?"

"When I dropped in the other night," he said with a sheepish grin. "Again, sorry for the whole leading those assholes to you, Gunner. I'll work to fix that. Anyway, when you kindly escorted me out, and I drove away, I noticed something shining from a nearby tree."

"And?"

"I drove a few blocks down the road, and then doubled back to make sure I wasn't seeing things. Sure enough, there was a man hidden up in that tree watching your place."

"What did you do?"

"I followed him, of course. I wanted to see who this guy was," Conor said. "When it began to lighten up outside, he climbed down, picked up his bag, and walked on the sidewalk like he was out for an early morning stroll or some shit."

"Professional. What did he look like?" Brick asked.

Conor reached for his pocket, and in a flash, guns were pulled. The PI froze. "Shit, you guys are going to give a guy a heart attack," Conor yelled. "I'm not carrying. My gun is in my glove box."

"You need to tell us when you're going to move, buddy. There've been too many bodies piling up on this case," Spence warned while lowering his weapon.

"Understood. My cell phone is in my right pocket. On there is a picture I managed to snap of the guy."

Rick huffed and stepped forward. "Like I asked before, Conor. Why don't you use your talents for good?" He reached into the pocket and pulled out his phone.

"That's what I'm trying to do," Conor said, and Spence sort of believed him.

"We need your fingerprint to unlock it," Rick said as he held the phone out.

Conor glanced around before saying, "I'm going to touch the phone, don't freak."

He lowered his hands and pressed his finger along a reader on the side of the phone.

"It's open. Is the photo in your gallery?" Rick asked.

"It should be one of the last ones."

Rick flipped through the pictures, and with a quick intake of breath, Spence knew it was one of Isabelle's men who'd approached Rick in the parking lot.

"That's him. That's the guy who tried to get me out of the SUV at the TV station."

"Shit, they've been watching us," Brick growled. "Where did they go?"

"A house in a swanky neighborhood."

"Premium Point?" Spence asked.

"Yeah. How'd you know?" Conor asked, looking confused.

"We're psychic," Brick said. "Gunner, Fletch, go back to the rental house and collect all our gear. Make sure you aren't followed. We'll set up a new base camp farther out of town."

"On it," Spence said as he brought his phone to life. "I'll have something within thirty minutes."

"As for you, Conor O'Brian, you're coming with us," Brick ordered.

"What?"

"Until we're sure which side you're on, we need to keep an eye on you. If it turns out you're not bullshitting us, no harm, no foul, and you're on your way. If you're working for those sick fucks who messed with kids' genetics, then all bets are off."

"Genetics?" Conor asked, and he looked confused, but they had to be sure. "I thought you were working on a missing person."

Rick walked up to him and said, "So did we."

\*\*\*

*Rick*

The new rental house was a cottage and a hive of activity. This time they weren't taking any chances and set up sensors in layers starting with the outer perimeter and working their way in. If anyone so much as looked in the direction of the cottage, they'd know, or at least that's how it felt to Rick.

They'd pulled up the floor plan of the house inside Premium Point, and the plans for the entire neighborhood. Since it was a gated and guarded community, Conor hadn't been able to follow the car past the entrance gates. Apparently, late that evening, he'd sent a drone into the community to see if he could find the car again. When he did, he took video surveillance of the house and yard, and he was able to look through a few windows where the drapes were open. He'd downloaded the footage and gave it to Spence.

"You weren't operating the drone that followed us into the community?" Spence asked as he looked at the file.

"It could've been. I was out there a couple of nights trying to get a lay of the land. If I did, it'd be on those video recordings."

Conor had been helpful so far, but there was still that nagging suspicion lingering he could be setting them up. Spence had torn the guy's past apart looking for anything that might suggest what side he was on, but he was clean other than a shocking number of parking tickets.

"Why don't you pay for parking?" Rick had to ask. The tickets, though paid, added up to a substantial amount.

"Because a lot of the time no one other than the parking patrol notices the ticketed abandoned vehicles in parking lots. I'll leave my car at a stakeout for a couple of days, gather surveillance footage from all the onboard cameras, and come pick it up before it's booted, and no one's the wiser."

"Not bad, but expensive."

"The client pays for it."

"Is that what you did with me?" Gunner asked. "Did they pay you?"

Conor stood and said, "No. You weren't hiding and easy to find. I haven't even cashed the damn check."

"Yeah, because I didn't think some asshole would be following me. I'm not a criminal."

"I told you, I'm sorry for leading your extended family to you. Somehow, I'll make this right for you," Conor said, standing toe to toe with Gunner.

"How?"

"I don't know yet, but it'll come to me."

Gunner huffed and walked away.

"Good luck," Spence said as he turned on the footage.

They watched as the drone traveled from Conor's car, through the high hedges, and eventually over a tall fence. For a long time, the drone flew down street after street searching for the right vehicle, and then the team's SUV came on the screen, but the drone kept going. Then the drone stopped over top a long driveway hovering over the car below.

"That's the vehicle the man was driving. I matched the license plates, though when I looked them up, they came back owned by a retired woman in her eighties named Ruth Everly."

"That's not the only strange thing. The boat getaway was a ruse. They had a house in the community to work out of, but didn't want anyone to know. They were probably back at their place before the shooting began and police arrived," Spence said.

"Wait, I heard the sirens and flew the drone out of there shortly after finding the car. I read in the news two people died that night. That was you guys?"

"Not the killing part. We were there investigating a disappearance," Brick said.

"Is that how this missing person turned into more?"

"We were called in by local PD to help search for a missing girl," Brick explained. "What we found is more. That's all you need to know."

"I can live with that." Conor nodded.

"You're going to have to," Spencer shot back. No one was happy this guy did what he did to Gunner, and the team had long memories.

The next drone footage was from above the house, and the car was gone.

"I came back and mapped the area."

They watched as the drone went from corner to corner, side to side, in a grid pattern. It stopped in front of a two-door shed in the backyard and then tried to peer inside the windows, but they were smudged and dirty. The drone approached the house, but drapes covered most windows. After searching, the drone found one window with the drapes pulled back. It hovered for a moment before getting closer.

"How quiet is your drone?" Rick asked.

"Silent. I gotta guy over in Jersey who does it up nice for me."

Rick felt like he was watching a horror movie, and was waiting for someone to jump out at any moment with a chainsaw. The drone neared the window and the video zoomed in, revealing a bedroom. A figure was sitting at a desk, but whoever it was had their back to the camera.

"Can you lighten that?" Brick asked.

"Yeah." Spence made the screen lighten.

The figure was a woman who had curly brown hair.

"Isabelle Noah?" Rick asked.

"Dorothy Rask as she wants to be known. It has to be her," Fletch said.

Rick sat back in his chair and said, "That's how she disappeared so quickly after retrieving Commander Rask's body. She didn't need to get out of town. She was only blocks away from the killings."

"The commander was going to come clean about the second child right before he was shot," Spence stated.

"That's why they silenced him," Shaw said.

"Wait, what's that?" Rick asked as he noticed something lying on the desk. "Can you make it bigger?"

As the object got larger, Rick could make out a few words. "It's a receipt from Big Apple Storage, unit forty-two."

"Holy shit," Fletch said. "You may've just blown this case wide open."

"How do you mean?" Rick asked.

Fletch wiggled his brow. "What type of things would a murderous geneticist have tucked away in private?"

"I don't know, but I sure as hell want to find out," Spence said.

"We need to find this place," Conor announced as if he were part of the team.

"Curb your enthusiasm. You haven't been cleared," Brick was quick to remind him.

"C'mon. I'm trying to help here."

"No matter what you say, it's not going to change anything. Trust is earned," Gunner harrumphed.

Conor slumped on the chair like a deflated balloon.

"It'll take time," Rick said.

Conor smiled and shrugged. "They're stuck with me until I repay my debt to Gunner."

"You're really taking that seriously?"

"Yeah. I wronged him, and I've gotta fix it," Conor said. "That's the way my *Maimeo* raised me."

"*Maimeo*?" Rick asked.

"It's pronounced Mam-o, which means grandmother in Irish."

"Your grandmother raised you?"

"It's a long story."

"Which we don't have time for now," Spence said as he joined the conversation. "We need to rest before we move."

"Move where?" Conor asked.

"Wouldn't you like to know," Gunner said as he came to stand over Conor. "You're with me. I'll be keeping an eye on you until this is over."

Rick grabbed Spence's forearms. "I could take a nap."

"Follow me." Spence chuckled as he led Rick upstairs to the second floor. "I've commandeered this room for us. It has its own bathroom."

"My hero. In the mood to join me for a shower?"

Spence gave him a look that could've melted a glacier.

\*\*\*

*Rick*

Rick leaned into the hard spray. The water was hot and soothing, and he felt his muscles starting to relax. He had almost everything he'd wanted except his Navy SEAL.

"Yo," Rick yelled.

"On my way," Spence hollered, and moments later, he appeared in the doorway, naked. "I had to respond to that lead on Dr. Frauste."

Rick eyed him up and down, then licked his lips. "That's okay," he rasped.

Spence walked into the shower and released a hiss. "Is it hot enough for you?"

"This is warm, not hot," Rick argued. "Aren't you SEALs supposed to be used to the water?"

"Cold and frigid water, and sometimes, if we're lucky, piss-warm water. I can assure you we don't go diving into any hot springs," Spence said with a laugh.

Rick was becoming addicted to the sound of Spence's laughter. He took it as a sign of happiness. He liked to think it was because of him, and gave himself a mental pat on the back.

"Why are you so smug?" Spence asked, undoubtedly noticing Rick's smile.

"Because you're happy," Rick stated. Seeing the shadows around Spence lift had Rick thinking of their future. "I love you."

"I love you too."

He'd never really allowed himself to have a future or make plans for one until recently.

"We should take a trip," Rick stated.

"A trip? To where?"

"Anywhere, I don't care. I've never had one."

"You mean like a vacation?" Spence asked as he moved over and pulled Rick into his arms. "You've never taken a trip for a holiday?"

"No. Do you take them?" Rick asked. "I've never felt safe enough to wander far."

"I have, but not in a while. Where would you like to go?"

Spence explored Rick's body, his hands rubbing tight muscles and leaving a trail of fire along the way.

"Tell me where you haven't been."

Spence blew out a long breath. "I've covered a lot of ground." He tilted his head as if he was going around the globe in his mind. "How about Portugal? I've never been there."

"Oh, that sounds perfect. Lots of coastline."

"As soon as this case is done and Simon has been dealt with, we'll make plans."

"It could take a while to find him. He's slimy. Believe me, I know."

"Trust me. We've found slimier, nastier, and cagier. We'll get him, and then you and I are taking a much-needed break."

Spence leaned in and began kissing the side of Rick's neck, sending all holiday thoughts flying out the window and replacing them with the wonderful sensations he was experiencing in the here and now. The feel of his lover's strong, muscled body against his own was enough to make Rick hard. Add in Spence's talented lips and tongue, and Rick was a goner.

Moans replaced words as Rick arched his neck in a desperate attempt to get closer to the sensation. Spence chuckled but never stopped his ministrations, increasing the heat with a few playful nibbles on Rick's collarbone and pecs.

Rick ran his hands over his lover's firm thighs on his way to the prize: Spence's thick cock. With the slide of Rick's hands, the big guy groaned, which was music to his ears. Rick turned his body to fully face Spence, causing the water to cascade over the both of them, further heating his skin and heightening his pleasure.

Spence slid his calloused hands over Rick's back, sending trails of electricity down his spine and straight to his throbbing balls. He dove in for a kiss Spence quickly mastered, leaving Rick breathless and needy. The onslaught continued until he couldn't take it any longer.

"Need you inside me," Rick moaned, and seconds later, he was rising into the air.

He grabbed a towel as an afterthought as Spence carried him to the bed. Rick never thought he'd be into being carried. Damn, it was hot.

Rick threw the bath towel down onto the bed to catch some of the water still on them before Spence laid him down, pressing his body weight on him. If his balls could explode, that move would've done it.

Rick was ready to explode and was desperately trying to hold on.

"Babe, I'm triggered and ready to blow," Rick admitted. "We need to slow down."

Spence looked down at him with a wild grin. "Sweetheart, you know I can make you come again."

"Yeah, but you need rest for tonight."

"You leave that to me."

And he did.

Rick's world was turned upside down before his lover groaned one last time before collapsing on the bed beside him. The sounds of their ragged breaths filled the room, and he couldn't move if he wanted to.

# CHAPTER TWENTY-ONE

*Spence*

After talking to the police chief, the local LEOs agreed they would assist the team with the raid on Isabelle Noah's house. The PI, Gunner, Rick, and Spence checked out the storage facility.

They'd been watching the storage yard and buildings for over two hours and noticed only one security guard wandering by with headphones on. They didn't expect much resistance out of him. There was no sign of dogs, and surveillance cameras were placed only at the front of the building and angled over the sliding drive-in gate.

"Okay, unit forty-two is what we're after," Gunner whispered. "If we get separated for any reason, head back here to the rendezvous point."

"If we have a warrant, why are we sneaking in?" Rick asked.

"Because we don't know if anyone at the facility is involved. We can get held up out front serving the search warrant, giving a co-conspirator enough time to get to the unit and destroy what's in it."

"Never thought of that," Rick said as he shook his head.

"You can't trust anybody," Gunner responded, glaring at the PI.

"I get it. You don't have to hammer me over the head." Conor huffed and leaned back in his seat.

"You're the one who came to us." Spence then continued laying out the plan. "Gunner and Conor will keep an eye on the front to ensure we don't have any unexpected visitors. Rick and I will enter the complex and locate unit forty-two."

The group split up and headed for their assigned destinations. Rick followed Spence's every move. He was thankful Arthur had taken the time to teach him how to use a gun, which he was now carrying, but he was clear he'd use it only in an emergency. Experienced, he was not.

Spence stopped beside the chain-link fence surrounding the storage buildings and took out his wire cutters, which went through metal like a hot knife on butter. He could hear a dog howling his fool head off in the distance, but, so far, nothing else pricked his senses. He held back, watching for any sign they'd been seen, as Spence cut through the fence and motioned him forward. When they were both clear, they ran to the closest building for cover.

Gunner's voice came into his concealed earpiece. "Confirmation, the raid has begun. Boots are on the ground."

Spence looked at Rick to make sure he understood: the clock started now. They had to get to the unit before anyone had a chance to destroy the information in the storage unit, especially since Isabelle Noah would realize she was trapped and whatever the storage unit held had to be removed to protect her.

Spence sped up as they took opposite sides of the alley between storage units, trying to find a number.

"I got eighty-six," Rick said over his mic. "Heading down the row now."

"Coming up right behind you," Spence alerted him as they jogged down the row.

"It has to be on this side because the numbers are going down, and they're even," Rick said as he pointed to the left.

"Got it."

They carried on as the numbers lowered and were nearing forty-two when the piercing screech of an alarm sounded above their heads.

"What the hell?" Rick froze.

"I need eyes," Spence said, and there was a quick response.

"The guard received a phone call and hit the alarm," Gunner stated. "I've got two headed your way. We'll deal with this dickhead."

"On it." Spence turned to find Rick farther down the building standing in front of one of the storage units.

"It's this one," he said. "I found it."

"Get down. We have company," Spence ordered as two men came in from the opposite direction.

Rick dove to the ground behind the edge of a second building just before bullets sprayed the wall. These were no ordinary security guards. Practiced and precise, they used hand signals indicative of military training. Spence figured these were working for Isabelle. How the fuck did they know to be here?

Spence returned fire, catching one of the men in the leg and taking him to the ground while the other disappeared in the darkness. Spence prayed Rick stayed down under cover until he had the chance to flush out the second man. Better yet, Spence hoped Rick had gone back to the rendezvous point, but knowing Rick, that wasn't likely.

Spence pressed his back against the concrete block wall and edged forward, trying to get a look at the guy he'd shot in the leg, but found no one. The second shooter must've dragged him off. That meant there were two armed men still out there while Rick was unprotected. That knowledge had him rethinking his attack. He started to prepare for hand-to-hand combat in close quarters. He lost the extra weight of his pack, choosing to carry his Glock and his knife as he sank low and began hunting.

***

*Rick*

Rick could hear the blood rushing through his veins. He wasn't in the military, and he'd never trained for field combat of any kind. Even with the odds against him, he refused to freak out or cower.

Spence was out there with two shooters who had one objective: prevent anyone from taking what was in that storage unit. At the same time the thought entered his mind, the smell of smoke hit him. *Shit.*

He scanned his immediate area, knowing he wouldn't see the flames as he was behind the back side of the building. He couldn't let them burn all that evidence. All the suffering Isabelle Noah had caused must come to light.

*Okay, find a defensible position.* He'd learned a lot while he'd lived on the streets, and he'd paid attention when the team was planning ops.

Rick sucked in a deep breath, scanned the area one more time, and backed out of his position so he could stand. Bullets continued to ricochet off the building to his left, and he remembered those being storage units numbered in the hundreds. He went right.

Low and slow, he moved across the back of the building until he found a ladder attached to the building. He climbed until he found himself in an old HVAC storage unit on the roof where the actual HVAC unit should be, but it looked long gone. The space was a good four feet by two feet and no one would be able to see him up there if he crouched.

He'd hunkered down where he'd have eyes on the storage unit they'd come for. He peered over the edge of the metal box and adjusted his stance until he had a clear view of the entire alley containing unit forty-two. This could work, but he'd feel better if he could see Spence. Out of the corner of his eyes, he caught movement to the left out and refocused his attention there. After a few minutes, his patience was rewarded.

A man in black sat behind an industrial recycling bin, dressing what looked to be a leg wound. Rick hoped someone was listening as he used his new bone mic to reach out to the team.

"I've got one bad guy shot in the leg positioned behind a recycling bin numbered twenty-five."

"Copy." He hadn't expected a reply but was damn happy to have one. He wasn't alone. He had a team.

Rick continued watching as one moment the shooter was applying a tourniquet to slow the bleeding, and the next, he was gone, pulled out of sight, and hopefully restrained.

The high-pitched ping of bullets ricocheting off the building to his right grabbed his attention as he saw Gunner working to unit forty-two, which now had smoke coming out of it. From what he could see, the fire was still small, but it could catch and destroy all the evidence in a matter of minutes. They had to find the other children from the program.

He tracked the shots aimed at Gunner to a shed sitting at the end of the row.

"Shed, end of the row same side as unit forty-two," he transmitted.

Gunner changed course, and Rick watched as the big man moved with lightning speed around an outer building as he closed in on the shed. Another round of shots sounded, and Rick watched in horror as Gunner fell to the ground. A split second later, the man who'd tried to force Rick out of the truck the day Donald was killed walked around the corner and pointed his gun directly at Gunner's head.

Rick stood and aimed his gun at the shooter and pulled the trigger. At the same time, Conor ran out from behind the bushes and threw his body over Gunner. Rick's shot missed, but it distracted the guy long enough for Spence to jump behind him and take him to the ground.

Both sprang up onto their feet as Spence skillfully knocked the gun out of the henchman's hand while delivering a blow to his jaw. The guy backed off a few feet, but he was still too close to Spence for Rick to take another shot. Isabelle's man pulled a knife from his belt and slashed it in the air in front of Spence as he produced his own.

They jockeyed for position, then the man kicked the ground and sent gravel flying into Spence's face. He moved to protect his eyes, and the asshole jabbed his knife, catching Spence in the shoulder. Rick couldn't look away or fire his gun. By the time he climbed down and rounded the building, the fight would be over.

Spence ignored his bleeding shoulder and continued to fight, going on the offensive with a combination of quick, sharp moves Rick had seen him practice at the lake house. He had the guy backing away from him, and he didn't let up until the other man let out a fierce cry and lunged at Spence with his knife held high. Spence angled his body, and when the guy thrust out, Spence rolled his to the left and came up behind the asshole, sinking his blade deep into his side.

The guy collapsed to the ground and stopped moving.

Rick lowered his gun and stared down at Spence as he stood alone with a bloody knife in his hand. The look on his face was something Rick would never forget: absolute calm in the face of the chaos raining down around them.

The world froze for a moment as they locked onto each other. This was the man he loved. He smiled.

Things moved fast after that. Police began arriving along with firetrucks and the rest of the team. Luckily, Gunner suffered only a flesh wound and a concussion. As for the PI, after sacrificing himself to protect Gunner, he stuck to the periphery while the cops and firefighters did their thing.

Once the fire department cleared the unit, they found it crammed full of bank boxes with files covering over fifty years of Frauste's and Isabelle's "experiments." The fire had charred only a small percentage of a massive amount of information. Rick couldn't believe they'd been so stupid. He would've scanned all the paperwork onto a laptop not connected to the internet, then he would've stored the information on various thumb drives and discs, hiding them in lock boxes in offshore locations known for their secrecy. Hubris had convinced Frauste and Noah that no one would look in a dingy storage unit for the wealth of information the team had uncovered.

The EMTs loaded the second shooter into an ambulance, a police officer accompanying his prisoner to the hospital.

When the rest of the team had breached Isabelle Noah's location, they found her sitting in a chair in her office with a single gunshot wound through her right temple, the gun on the ground below her right hand. Rick saw it as a coward's way out, and it deprived all the people she'd harmed the satisfaction of seeing justice done. An argument could be made for keeping the afflicted from having to relive the horror, and at least Noah was dead. Frauste would have to be dealt with.

Those experiments had real-world consequences. People's lives were irreparably altered as they were victimized in the most horrific way. Rick couldn't help but wonder what happened to Elise's first child, the boy she was told died during birth. He had to be out there somewhere, likely blind to the events over the past four weeks.

When the team finally made it back to the rental, they collapsed onto chairs, couches, and pillows on the living room floor, decompressing. Rick sat securely in Spence's arms, where he intended to stay for the foreseeable future. The wound to Spence's shoulder had required eight stitches but would heal without lasting damage. The memory of the fight would live forever in Rick's mind.

After all the statements were taken and the reports filed, Spence was quiet. Tomorrow they'd start to dig through the mass of files they'd found. As for today, all Rick wanted to do was shut down with his lover.

"Okay, the next time we catch a missing person's case, we're throwing it back," Gunner stated from the couch, his arm in a sling and head bandaged with Conor still by his side.

"Agreed," everyone said in unison.

Rick hadn't been this physically and emotionally drained in years, and he knew it would take time to recharge. All he wanted right now was twenty-four hours of peace.

The quiet was broken moments later by the sound of Billy Joel belting out "Uptown Girl" from Rick's phone.

"Seriously, that's your new ringtone?" Shaw asked with a chuckle.

"Yep, and it's fabulous," Rick shot back.

"Glad to see some things will never change." Spence laughed.

Rick gave his boyfriend a quick kiss before answering the call. "Hello."

"Hello, is this Rick with L. H. Investigations?" a woman's voice asked.

Rick's chest puffed out a little and he said, "Yes, this is Rick."

"Hi. This is Rosaline."

# CHAPTER TWENTY-TWO

*Spence*

Spence and Rick had doubled back twice and changed directions repeatedly to ensure they weren't being followed. When they'd made their way to the rendezvous point, the rest of the team hung back out of sight, keeping an eye out because if he and Rick didn't catch the tail, they would.

Rick'd received the call out of the blue, and Spence hadn't seen it coming. The dust hadn't even had time to settle, but this was the way of things when an op was in play. Things moved fast, and everyone had to be prepared for the unexpected.

Spence knew he hadn't heard the last of this when it came to the Navy. Someone would be in touch sooner or later, but for now, this was the last piece of the case that needed to be put to rights.

"It's over there," Rick said as they pulled into a parking lot some twenty miles from where they'd started.

The mall looked to be packed with shoppers carrying on with their lives, unknowing how thin the line between their orderly world and chaos truly was. He spotted the gray van near the rear of the lot and parked beside it.

"We're doing the right thing here," Rick said as he took hold of Spence's hand. "I'm positive."

He'd never been one to require reassurance, but Rick's touch settled something inside of him as nothing had ever before, and he allowed himself to feel it.

"Yeah, we are," Spence agreed. "Something good has to come out of all this, and I'm happy we could help."

Rosaline stepped out of the van's driver's seat and walked to the front of the van, where she waited for them.

"Let's go get this done," Rick stated. He wanted to kiss Spence and tell him he loved him, but it wasn't the time or the place. But with one look, Spence let Rick know they were of the same mind.

Spence reached for his door handle and stepped out into the midday sun. He was exhausted, and his shoulder hurt like hell, but he would've dragged himself to be here if he had to.

This was the reward, if there truly was one.

\*\*\*

*Rick*

Rick stepped outside their SUV and allowed the day's warmth to calm him. He loved the sun and immediately felt better when he was out in it. He'd admit to being nervous. After the night he'd had, he figured it would take a while before he got his sea legs back under him.

Gripping the envelope, Rick walked over to the sliding back door of the van while Spence took position outside with Rosaline. The door opened and Rick came face-to-face with Ellen Hammon.

"Hello. I'm Rick," he said as he held out his hand, but instead of taking his hand, she leaned down and hugged him tight before bursting into tears. "It'll be all right. From this point forward, you'll have a new life. Trust me when I tell you, I know how hard it is to start over, but it's worth it. You're going to be happy again. I promise."

Ellen released him and retreated into the van to allow Rick to sit inside. When he got a good look at the girl, he could see the fear and uncertainty in her expression. She was pale, maybe five foot two, skinny, with long dark hair.

Rick noticed she kept tugging down her long-sleeve shirt over her hands. "Someday that won't be your reality." He'd worn his khaki shorts for this exact reason and lifted the hem only an inch above his knee where his cutting began. "These will no longer define you."

Ellen looked at his healed scars and cautiously revealed her arms. The red lines and healing cut marks were like stepping back in time. He knew those emotions well.

"You're a young woman who's been given a chance to remake yourself into whoever you want to be. The same as I did when I was young."

"You ran away too?" Ellen asked, and Rick knew she was searching for a connection.

"No. I was thrown out. But we ended up in the same place, alone and scared. You have Rosaline to guide you. She's a remarkable and kind woman who will teach you how to carry on and thrive."

"I love her." Ellen smiled when she glanced out the front window at her surrogate mom. Then she sobered and asked, "Do you think I'm a monster?"

He knew that feeling well. "You are not a monster. I've met monsters, and I can guarantee you are not among them."

"But they made me like they did Frankenstein's monster."

Rick could understand the comparison, and it certainly had a ring of truth, but not the way this poor child thought. "They were the monsters, not you. You're the beautiful, smart, strong young woman you've always been. Knowing what happened doesn't change who you are and who you'll become."

He lifted the large envelope and said, "You have the power to create the person you want to be."

"How did you get away from your past?" Ellen asked, sounding every bit the teenager. "It's always there in my head."

"I reinvented myself with the help of a kind person. I changed my name, got my education, worked hard, and made a solid, happy life for myself. It took time for me to *feel* who I'd made myself into, but I did it and so can you. You're fortunate you have Rosaline. She'll be there for you as you navigate the road you'll make for yourself. You're young and have help from me and my team. We won't fail you."

Ellen reached into her pocket, pulled out a thumb drive, and handed it to Rick. "This is for you. It was my da—it's Tom's book. I burned the paper copy."

"Thank you. We'll take care of it from this point on. It's foolish to tell you to forget your life up until now. The better way to look at it is to take what you know and make it yours. Be who you want to be, knowing you have the power to shape your life." He handed her the envelope and watched as she opened it. "From this moment on, Ellen Hammon is missing and presumed dead."

Her shaking hands fumbled with the identification inside. She pulled out a driver's license and said, "Christine Rehez. Rosaline's last name." She leaned forward and squeezed his hand. "You know, I haven't got a license to drive yet."

"Well, we took some liberties, but swear you'll have Rosaline teach you before you get out on the road."

She smiled. "I swear I won't drive until I have lessons." Christine held out her pinky and Rick hooked his pinky around it. "Pinky promise." The move helped to remind him just how young and innocent this girl was.

"Good. Now there's your new Social Security number, birth certificate, proof of immunization, doctor records, school transcripts, and all the documentation you'll need to go forward with your life. Also, there's money to help you start over again."

"Thank you for everything you and your team have done for me. I never thought people like you existed outside books."

Rick felt his heart skip a beat at her kind words. "There are decent, honest people out there, and you'll be one of them. Who knows, someday someone might need you to help them."

At that moment, Rick realized he'd come full circle in his life, and was in the position to give back. Christine Rehez would benefit from everything he'd lived through to get to this place. From here on, she could fill her life with hopes and dreams as the shadow of what was done to her became a memory that'd fuel her recovery.

"I will help people," she said through shaky tears. "I want my life to mean more than an experiment in some lab. I'm me. My name is Christine, and I'm my own person."

"You certainly are."

# CHAPTER TWENTY-THREE

*Simon*

Simon walked into his office and threw his phone at the wall. "Where the hell are you, Spike?"

He'd sent the idiot out days ago to retrieve his property, and neither Spike, Adam—or Rick, as he was called these days—had shown up since. This shit wouldn't be tolerated. He'd send out five more of his guys to get his point across. No one escaped from him. No matter how many years it took to track down that street rat. He'd have his revenge as he squeezed the life out of him with his bare hands.

It'd be a lesson to the others who looked at Adam as some kind of hero for making it out. If they took off, Simon would hunt them down, but he'd be spending money while hemorrhaging money. He threw himself into his leather chair and pushed one of the buttons on his desk phone.

"Come on, answer the damn phone," Simon grumbled as he tried to reach his second-in-command. "Where the fuck is everyone today?" He slammed his fist down on the desk. Someone would pay for this.

"All alone?" a voice said from the open doorway. "Need a friend?"

Simon looked up to find the object of his rage standing before him. "Well, well, well. Look who's come crawling back. Hoping for leniency, I'm sure. Pathetic as always, Adam."

Adam took two steps into the room, and Simon noticed something different about him. "My name is Rick."

***

*Rick*

As recently as a month ago, Rick would've been terrified to be standing here. Now, he felt nothing but disgust at the human garbage sprawled behind his desk.

"Adam, Rick, what does it matter? You'll be dead soon enough." Simon laughed as he pulled open the top right drawer of his desk. He frowned, opened the drawer below it, and switched to the other side and snarled as he searched in both those drawers.

"Looking for this?" Rick asked as he held up a plastic evidence bag containing a gun. "I wonder how many crimes can be linked to this one piece of metal. The things forensics can do these days are amazing."

Simon pushed another button on his office phone, not receiving an answer as Rick knew he wouldn't.

"You shouldn't've come looking for me. I'm not the frightened boy I used to be." Rick grinned as he took two more paces into the room. "That was your mistake. When I was a kid, you had power over me. Took advantage of me, and I'm here to rectify that."

Simon struck out his arm, clearing off the desk and sending the items crashing onto the floor before standing. "Who do you think you are coming in here making threats? You're nothing but a dirty little street rat who likes to get fucked for money. You're nothing. I have dozens of guys just like you out there waving their asses and making me money."

"Oh, you mean like some of these young men?"

Eight of Simon's "boys" walked through the open door and took up positions by Rick's side. Simon looked ready to swallow his tongue.

"What the hell are you rats doing here? Get back to your posts before I have you beaten," Simon threatened. But no one moved, and Rick watched as the realization hit Simon. He was alone. "Where are my men?"

"Busy saving their asses by selling you out." Rick chuckled. The juxtaposition of their positions felt strange and satisfying. Instead of being trapped, scared, and alone, Rick held all the power, and it was his tormentor's turn to be put in his place. "How does it feel knowing no one is coming to save you?"

Simon's eyes shifted from side to side, obviously looking for a way out. Rick handed the bagged gun to the kid beside him and took two paces forward. If Simon was going to take on somebody, it would be him.

"As I said, it was a stupid, stupid move." Rick shook his head at the pathetic excuse of a human before him. "But I'm glad now you came looking for me. At least I'll have years enjoying knowing you'll be rotting in prison for a long, long time." Simon's lip raised in a snarl. "Don't worry. You'll have plenty of friends in prison. Why, with your slim build, you'll have plenty of attention in no time."

That did it. Simon's eyes bulged, and he lunged at Rick, who easily twisted out of the way.

"You see, my new friends whom you threatened to hurt if I didn't come back taught me a few things."

"I'll fucking kill you," Simon yelled as he came at him again.

This time Rick didn't avoid the confrontation; he engaged the enemy. With a dive and sweep of his leg, Rick had Simon on the ground to the cheers of the boys. Before Simon could stand up, Rick drove his knee into the asshole's back, right between the shoulder blades. Simon collapsed onto the ground with a deep groan of pain as the room filled with part of the team and the Chicago PD.

Rick soon found himself in Spence's strong arms. "I'm so proud of you. But that isn't ever happening again. I almost had a heart attack waiting outside while Simon was angling to kill you."

"I'm all right. Everything will be okay now," Rick assured as he hugged his lover close. "He won't be able to hurt anyone anymore."

"Damn right," Gunner said as he walked by dragging a handcuffed, groaning, and now former pimp/small-time crime boss from the room to a waiting squad car.

Conor wasn't far away, making sure Simon remained docile. The dude was never far from Gunner, and Rick couldn't help but wonder if he planned on returning to Fire Lake with them.

Spence pulled something from his pocket and handed it to Rick.

"What's this?" Rick asked as he turned the envelope over in his hands.

"Open it."

Rick looked around at the emptying office, shrugged, and tore open the seal. When he looked inside, he found airline tickets. Pulling them out to read them, Rick got a strange, heavy feeling in his stomach.

"Portugal," Rick said, and his hands began shaking.

"I thought we'd start in Lisbon, then drive up the coast to Porto. Lounge around on the beach, eat amazing food... And I'm sure we'll find plenty else to do." Spence smiled.

Rick hugged Spence tight. "Oh yeah, we will."

# EPILOGUE

Cheryl Lowell sat back in her cushioned lounger, sipping on her morning mimosa over breakfast as the new pool boy scrubbed the Italian marble stairs leading into her new thirty-six-thousand-gallon pool. Of course, the stairs didn't need cleaning, but why eat without a show. And what a handsome, muscled twenty-year-old show it was.

As she sat under her cotton-draped cabana with the breeze softly blowing, she couldn't imagine her life any other way. They'd be having dinner at the club later, giving her a chance to debut the new diamond choker she'd received on her birthday from her wealthy husband. What he lacked in virility and youth was more than made up for by the size of his wallet, and soon enough, he'd be six feet under, leaving her the grieving widow of a billionaire. Who cared if the man made his money on the backs of cheap labor in third-world countries and lined every pocket to protect his interests right up to the U.S. Senate?

Her life was exactly where she'd expected it to be. Here she was, forty-two, gorgeous, toned, powerful, and rich. Perhaps she'd summer in Florence this year.

"You missed a spot." She pointed to a rather deep corner on the second staircase.

The boy nodded with a shy grin and dutifully bent over, sticking his bright red Speedo-covered ass into the air.

Yes. That was much better.

"Excuse me, ma'am, but these arrived for you." Her maid, Ann, approached the cabana.

"Can't you see I'm enjoying my breakfast?" Cheryl snapped without looking at the woman.

Ann replied, "Yes, ma'am," while glancing at the pool.

Cheryl turned to find Ann holding a vase full of flowers with a note attached. "Bring them here."

She examined the bouquet filled with roses, lilies, gerberas, orchids, and the usual greenery. But when she came across a stray carnation, she plucked it from the bunch and threw it on the ground where it belonged.

"How pedestrian." If someone was going to send her flowers, they had to be top of the line, none of the common varieties.

Ann held out the note attached, and Cheryl finished her drink before reaching for the little envelope. "Set those somewhere I am not," she ordered and snatched it out of Ann's hand.

"Yes, ma'am."

When Ann was gone, Cheryl opened the small envelope, wondering who was trying to curry favor with her this time. She pulled out the card to read the single line.

*Happy Mother's Day*
*from Adam Jefferson*

She scrunched up her nose. This had to be a joke. She'd never had children. They weren't part of the plan. They were little more than money-sucking life destroyers, and she'd do nothing to ruin her figure.

However, there was that one short time in her life... But he was only a stepson. Not hers, and long gone. She'd made sure of it.

As she put the card aside, wholly unconcerned with someone's rude idea of a joke, a commotion by the house caught her attention. She stood to see what was happening to find several men in suits flashing badges and pushing their way into the backyard.

"Cheryl Lowell, we have a warrant for your arrest," the first man said as he stepped into her impeccably white cabana with his dirty shoes.

"Take off your shoes," she yelled, making the man laugh.

"Lady, where you're going, my shoes are the least of your problems."

Her phone pinged with a text, and she looked down to find a message from her husband that read: "On a flight, tell them nothing."

Her ears began ringing as her carefully curated cabana was now filled with common people. It wasn't until her hands were being cuffed behind her back that she connected the dots.

She took one last look at the card and the lone carnation she'd thrown on the ground, now being trampled by the mass of people.

"Adam?"

Cheryl was pulled away from her beloved white cabana and pool boy as visions of the teenage boy she'd thrown onto the streets all those years ago flashed behind her eyes.

It couldn't be.

***

*Spence*

Spence looked down at his phone to read the incoming message. *Mission Complete.*

He deleted the message and shoved his phone into his pocket.

"Who was that?" Rick asked as the two of them sat on the large rock on the top of their island on Fire Lake. "Do you have to go?"

"Wrong number. Nothing to worry about."

"You know, if you can't tell me, it's okay to say you can't tell me. I understand you have certain aspects of your work that you can't share with me," Rick said as he leaned back into Spence's chest.

"Thank you for understanding," he said while hugging him.

Spence knew Rick wanted to move on and live his new life without anything holding him back, but that wasn't the way Spence rolled.

Rick with his sunny attitude was all about looking to the future, but that bitch who threw him out and caused all his pain had it coming, and then some. Spence wasn't alone in his thinking. The whole team had helped justice find its way to Cheryl's doorstep.

"I still can't believe we bought this island." Rick laughed as he looked out at the boats floating by. "But I'm happy we did."

"Me too," Spence said. "You deserve to have your own place to escape to whenever you need it."

"And so do you," Rick said with a smile that warmed every part of Spence.

"All I need is you," Spence said, meaning every word.

Wherever Rick was, was Spence's quiet space. Even if sometimes his lover talked a mile a minute, his soul was settled and calm with him, and the nightmares remained at bay. He knew someday he'd have to get all the crazy, messed-up shit out of his brain and go back into therapy, but this was his reward for all those years of service, and for now, he'd enjoy it.

Peace at last.

# ABOUT THE AUTHOR

M. Tasia is a M/M romance author who lives in Ontario, Canada. She's is a dedicated people watcher, lover of romance novels, 80's rock, and happily-ever-afters (once the MCs are put through their paces, of course), who grew up with a love of reading. She's a firm believer that everyone deserves to have love, excitement, and crazy hot romance in their lives. Love should be celebrated and shared.

### Connect with M.:

mtasiabooks.com
FB: mtasiabooks
twitter: @mtasiaauthor
IG: @m.tasia.author
TikTok: @mtasiauthor

www.BOROUGHSPUBLISHINGGROUP.com

If you enjoyed this book, please write a review. Our authors appreciate the feedback, and it helps future readers find books they love. We welcome your comments and invite you to send them to info@boroughspublishinggroup.com.

Follow us on Facebook, Twitter and Instagram, and be sure to sign up for our newsletter for surprises and new releases from your favorite authors.

Are you an aspiring writer? Check out www.boroughspublishinggroup.com/submit and see if we can help you make your dreams come true.

Love podcasts? Enjoy ours at www.boroughspublishinggroup.com/podcast

Made in the USA
Las Vegas, NV
02 October 2022

56372810R00114